MISSING SISTERS

MISSING SISTERS
Gregory Maguire

MARGARET K. McELDERRY BOOKS
New York
Maxwell Macmillan Canada
Toronto
Maxwell Macmillan International
New York Oxford Singapore Sydney

Margaret K. McElderry Books
Macmillan Publishing Company
866 Third Avenue
New York, NY 10022

Maxwell Macmillan Canada, Inc.
1200 Eglinton Avenue East
Suite 200
Don Mills, Ontario M3C 3N1

Macmillan Publishing Company is part of the Maxwell
Communication Group of Companies.
First edition
Printed in the United States of America
10 9 8 7 6 5 4 3 2 1
The text of this book is set in Caslon #540.
Maguire, Gregory.
Missing sisters / Gregory Maguire.
—1st ed.
p.   cm.
Summary: Twelve-year-old Alice, an orphan who has never been adopted
because of her physical handicap and difficult personality, is shocked to
discover she has an identical twin sister living nearby.
ISBN 0-689-50590-6
[1. Orphans—Fiction. 2.
Adoption—Fiction. 3. Twins—
Fiction. 4. Physically handicapped—Fiction.]
I. Title.
PZ7.M2762M1 1994
[Fic]—dc20   93-8300

+

M 276 m

For Debbie Kirsch, with love

CONTENTS

Part One
ICE AND FIRE

"Look. Lookit, Sister," said the girl. She stretched her hands out on either side of her. "It's raining out one window and snowing out the other."

"I'll look in a minute," said the nun. "After I get this oil off the burner—it's popping like nobody's business." She hustled the skillet onto the chopping board. "I'll burn this place to the ground yet."

"Oh, don't do that," said the girl.

"Pray that I don't," said the nun. "Say a prayer to the patron saint of stupid people, whoever that might be." She dried her pink hands on a square of burlap cut from a potato sack. "Now, what's to see, Alice?"

"Lookit: snow," said Alice, pointing out the large windows over the kitchen counter. Snow indeed. "And lookit: rain." Across the room and above the sink, the other windows were spattered with raindrops.

"Well, well," said the nun. "Fancy, you're right." She folded her arms across her apron bib for a moment in stillness, not like her. "Isn't it grand."

In the dawn storm the big kitchen of the retreat house seemed lit with purple. Alice was a twelve-year-old shadow, dark and observant, of ancient Sister Vincent de Paul, who in her black veil and habit and white apron looked like a witch in bandages. Slotted spoons and ladles and strainers hung from a central ring, a kind of chandelier of utensils. Flour from the day's bread-baking efforts drifted in the air between the windows, an inside weather of white dust. The room smelled of oil faintly scorching.

The other girls and the other sisters were still asleep. Alice thought of them in their beds in the dormitories. Seventeen girls snoring their vacation trip away, while only Alice Colossus was awake and listening. Alice and, of course, Sister Vincent de Paul, who with her bum foot clumped around in a huge shoe like a safe-deposit box.

"You're very sharp," said Sister Vincent de Paul. "You've a keen eye when you're on your own, Alice."

"I'm not on my own," said Alice. "You're here."

"You know what I mean." Sister Vincent de Paul went to the walk-in refrigerator for eggs. She planted her square shoe like a cinder block and swung the rest of her body around it. Her skirts swished. Alice tried hard to keep the sounds sure in her mind, for relishing: the thump of shoe, the rustle of black cotton, and behind it the hiss of the two-minded storm. Or perhaps it was the sizzle of oil she still heard. Alice loved to be Sister Vincent de Paul's helper before the house was up. It was her ears' clearest time of day.

"Think fast!" called Sister Vincent de Paul from the door, and threw a package of frozen blueberries across the room. Alice saw it before she heard it, but managed neatly to swipe it from the air before it landed on the floor. "Bravo!" chortled Sister Vincent de Paul and returned, *thump rustle thump rustle*, with two dozen eggs.

"Now tell me why you think the storm both rains and snows," said the nun, cracking eggs with one hand until twenty-four golden suns had flopped chummily in the flour.

"It can't make up its mind, like me," said Alice.

"Say it slower. Think your consonants."

"It—can't—make—up—its—mind," said Alice again. If Sister Vincent de Paul would look up, she could easily lip-read what she couldn't make out by sound. But Sister Vincent de Paul wouldn't lip-read Alice, because Alice was merely lazy and could do better if she tried.

"The storm can't make up its mind?"

It had been a joke, but it wasn't funny the second time. "Storm's stupid," said Alice.

"It's beautiful," Sister Vincent de Paul declared, poking out the eyes of the eggs with a slotted spoon till they bled yellow. "Are you going to grease those muffin tins?"

"Storm's mixed up," said Alice. "Like me."

"The storm," said Sister Vincent de Paul—and then a crash of thunder announced an opinion—"the storm is brilliant! Like you!" There was lightning, and more thunder. The snow was dancing in spirals. Around and down, more and more. The rain out the other window spattered all the harder.

"The line of snow cloud must be just above this room,"

said Sister Vincent de Paul, sprinkling a little flour onto the breadboard, lifting a spoon, and pointing heavenward. "It'll shift in a moment. We're at a miraculous juncture. As usual. Warm front and cold front having a stare down directly overhead. And only you and me to notice, Alice."

Alice missed some of this. She rubbed Crisco into the muffin tins. "It's just a cloud," she said.

"And you're just a girl, and life is just life," said Sister Vincent de Paul gaily. "And the morning bread just feeds us daily so we may notice such goings-on!" She began to sing in a sort of off-center way—her voice was riding the melody like a kid on a bicycle for the first time, whoopsing and wobbling along. "Then sings my soul, my Savior God, to Thee. How great Thou art, how great Thou art!"

Alice hummed a little to herself. The lightning stitched a path between snow and rain, the thunder kettle-drummed. The kitchen lights flickered and went out just as Sister Vincent de Paul was returning the pan of oil to the burner. "Oh," said Alice. "Mercy!" said Sister Vincent de Paul. The skillet bumped into the corner of the stove, and a long silver tongue of oil sloshed out. In a moment the counter was on fire. Small yellow-blue flames ran up the wall like morning glories growing on a trellis in a hurried-up nature movie.

"Salt," snapped Sister Vincent de Paul. Alice ran for the butler's pantry and came back with six saltshakers, not one of which held more than a teaspoon. She began to untwist the caps. "No, the salt in the canister!" said Sister Vincent de Paul, beating at the fire with her apron. Alice hadn't remembered the canister.

4

But salt didn't do it, and the fire extinguisher's help was only limp and sputtery. "Alice, you must run and wake everyone." Sister Vincent de Paul was yelling to be sure she was heard. "And call the fire brigade!"

Alice couldn't do the phone. For some reason she couldn't hear well over wires and through the little dots in the earpiece. So she stumbled through the swinging door and across the refectory, past the twenty-five places set at the two long tables. Skidded on the circle of braided rug in the hall and turned the corners on the big, carved staircase like a pro. Her long legs drew her up four steps at a time.

Rachel Luke and Esther Thessaly were coming back from the john together (they were supposed to call it the jane, since John was an evangelist and apostle, but nobody did). Sister Isaac Jogues was wafting up and down the corridor with her nose in her breviary, muttering matins. Hadn't they noticed the lights go off? "Ahh," said Alice. "Fire in the kitchen! Wake up!"

Rachel and Esther, who were only about eight, clutched each other and said, "What'd she say?" But Sister Ike dropped her breviary to the floor and strode like a line-backer down the corridor toward Alice. "Fire! Where, Alice?"

"Wake up, wake them up!" Alice said wildly, tearing from Sister Ike's grasp and turning into the older girls' dormitory. "Fire in the kitchen! Don't anyone hear me? *Fire*!"

The clock in the hall chimed six and three quarters. Alice could hear its bonging, like an angel's announcement of the hour of death. Domestic thunder. Sister Ike had roused Sister John Bosco, who appeared without her wimple, showing spikes of silver hair and putting to rest for all time the rumor that she was bald as a basketball. Alice had gabbled her message more and more clumsily at the groggy girls. In a tatter of nightgowns, habits, and even four-year-old Ruth Peters in her shameful soiled diapers, they lined up and counted themselves and marched single file down the right-hand side of the stairs, no talking and no running. Sister Francis of Assisi soon hoisted the sobbing Ruth in her arms, thinking nothing of the stink, or maybe just offering it up.

Sister John Bosco and Sister Francis Xavier had run on ahead to the kitchen, from which large balls of black smoke emerged and changed shape in the air. Alice said, "Phone!" but it turned out the phone lines had been cut, too, perhaps by the same tree limb that had downed the power lines.

They were unsure what to do. Outside it rained and snowed, back and forth like armies advancing and retreating, not only on the odd, steep roofs of the retreat house, but on the pine-toothed hills and stubbled meadows of the desolate country of God. There wasn't a farmhouse within a twenty-minute walk, and the hamlet with the fire station seemed so far away as to be in another century, beyond decades of snowdrift and ice. The city of Troy, where they usually lived, was like a past life, two hours away. "Girls, into your boots and coats," said Sister Jake, but where were they to go?

By the time the upstairs clock struck seven, all the girls, including Alice, were swaddled in wool coats and scarves and sweating like mad, standing in two rows just inside the French doors and floor-to-ceiling windows. You couldn't even see the lake, just fifty yards down the slope. Sister Jake kept counting the girls obsessively, as if one might be missing, but she came up each time with eighteen, which was the right number.

She called them by name. The girls had Old Testament first names and New Testament surnames; they were Sarahs and Ruths and Naomis and Miriams. Alice's first name, a quirk in the pattern, had come from a benefactress of the Sacred Heart Home for Girls, and her last name from St. Paul's letter to the Colossians. Alice Colossus.

Alice Colossus. A kind of grade-school Frankenstein orphan: tall, pretty deaf in a crowd, weird. While Sister Jake counted the girls, Alice counted the nuns.

The nuns had the names of men. Sister Francis Xavier, Sister Francis de Sales, Sister Francis of Assisi. (They all called each other Sister Frank, but no one else could.) Sister John Vianney. Sister Isaac Jogues. (Jake. Ike.) Sister John Bosco, the boss nun. (John Boss.) And of course Sister Vincent de Paul.

All seven sisters: three in the kitchen, four in the parlor.

Naomi Matthews, at fourteen the oldest girl, began to pray the rosary, loudly. The other girls took it up, the pattern of their voices familiar to Alice in the rhythm, though not in the meaning. *Braa* na na, na na *naa*, bra na na na NA. Sister Isaac Jogues told them to please hush up while they decided what to do. Naomi Matthews glared pityingly at Sister Ike's lack of faith in *God*, but dropped her voice.

Alice couldn't make out what they were jabbering over,

7

but she could guess some of the trouble. The diocesan bus they'd come in had gone back to Albany. They had one car, but the roads were surely slick with ice. If the whole building burned to the ground, what would they do?

"Boathouse," said Alice loudly, proving to Naomi and all that she hadn't been concentrating on the prayers. "Sister, we can hide in the boathouse."

"Alice, if it's important enough to be heard, it's important enough to say correctly." Even at a juncture of fire and brimstone, nuns couldn't resist the tart reproof.

"Safe in the *boathouse*."

Sister Ike's expression smoothed over: This was a possibility. Alice felt proud. Maybe she wasn't so holy, maybe she had failing grades in deportment because her speech was zigzaggy, but at least she was helpful.

The swinging doors of the kitchen flew open. From across the room they could see the disaster: The small, localized fire had just bloomed into an inferno. Sister Francis Xavier and Sister John Bosco emerged with little Sister Vincent de Paul between them. Her veil was on fire and the shoulders of her habit were also winged with orange, like tongues of flame at Pentecost. The girls stared at the sight, which reminded them of the Giotto in the math room, though they couldn't have named the painter.

Sister Francis Xavier threw Sister Vincent de Paul on the carpet and knocked chairs aside rolling around on top of her. Sister John Bosco saw the girls lined up inside the glass doors as if for a photo and screamed so loudly even Alice got it. "For the love of Christ, get out of here! There are gas lines in there, are you mad?"

They broke the single-file processional form and tumbled, screaming, out onto the porch. Slipping, holding hands, plunging, they skidded down the stone steps to the snowdrifts on the lawn. Without stopping for their coats, Sister John Bosco and Sister Francis Xavier followed, dragging Sister Vincent de Paul with them. They didn't stop till they got to the far edge of the lawn, where the day before the girls had made snowmen.

"Look," Sister John Bosco had said yesterday to her nuns, "all these snow creatures, look what they are. Not mothers and fathers and children, which I thought was universal. These look like snow orphans and snow nuns." And it seemed to be true: a polite line of snow orphans, black smiles made of raisins, and behind them a few scattered snow nuns, with crucifixes made of carefully broken twigs pressed into their modest, vaguely shaped fronts. But today, in the blizzard, the snow orphans and nuns were looking swollen and anonymous, their features blurred.

They had all just collected themselves near the stone shrine to Our Lady of Lourdes when the kitchen wing popped like a balloon. Glass shattered into the driveway. The roof was first crowned in flames and then disappeared in a screech just like a car crash; you could hear brakes squeal, metal scrape, giant iron fists punch each other inside out. Even Alice got it, both ears. All the while the snow whitened the day, and odd stabs of lightning and wrongheaded thunder kept up their tricks.

Alice broke the reestablished line to throw herself at Sister Vincent de Paul. The little woman's face was as black as her habit, with smoke and char, and her eyelashes were crinkled like a bug's legs. Her eyes were closed, her lips split and bleeding. What was left of her veil seemed to have melted into her head, and the skin of her scalp was red and raising in welts. Alice began to pick the flecks of veil out of her scalp, while she wept. But she was tearing the skin open, so she stopped; and Sister Francis Xavier stopped her, too, with a sharp remark.

They huddled under an apple tree and watched the place burn. It began to seem to be in slow motion. But maybe the rain and snow were being helpful, slowing down the damage? God's grace? The girls gazed, partly delighted at the crisis; the nuns seemed lost without little attention bells to rap or sour balls to award to the girls as bribes. But Naomi Matthews suddenly wrenched herself to her knees and cried out, pointing a mittened hand. The fire had arced itself over the main roof beam and descended like the teeth of the devil onto the roof of the chapel.

How could they have been so awful! They had saved themselves, but not the Blessed Sacrament. The sacred Hosts, the Body of Christ—it was too horrible. The girls took this in as fully as the nuns, and as deeply.

The three Sister Franks like a team of Green Berets all leaped up and began to run back to the chapel. Sister John Bosco was shouting wildly at them. She wagged a forbidding finger, but their black flapping skirts and veils pitched on through the snow. For the second time in half an hour Sister John Bosco swore in a most unchurchly fashion. She yelled at the girls that no one should under any circumstances move a muscle, and she headed after her disobedient sisters.

This left only Sister Isaac Jogues and Sister John Vianney with the unconscious Sister Vincent de Paul and eighteen schoolgirls. Naomi Matthews jumped up to run help the nuns save the sacred Hosts, signs of her Lord and Savior Jesus Christ, but Sister Isaac Jogues tackled her and sat on her to save her from a holy scorching. Sister Vincent de Paul was apparently martyr enough for one day. Naomi will never get over *this* disappointment, Alice observed to herself. Naomi Matthews wanted nothing so dearly as to die for her faith. She could be quite cross when kept from it.

But the main drama was past. Sister Francis of Assisi appeared at the chapel bearing the monstrance, its hammered gold sunrays oddly bright even across all that vacant whiteness. The other Sister Franks carried the Bible and the crucifix from the high altar and the small gold container called the ciborium that the communion Hosts were kept in. Sister John Bosco had gathered up the altar linen, a strange thing to save, the girls all thought, until they saw how she bound up Sister Vincent de Paul's head in it.

Then they sat in the boathouse, on top of the rowboats and canoes stored upside down for the winter. They sang hymns and prayed for Sister Vincent de Paul, while Sister Ike and Sister Francis de Sales braved the icy roads in the Dodge Dart, and went to get help. The girls had advanced to "Ninety-nine Bottles of Beer on the Wall," and the nuns to leading calisthenics to keep them all warm, when help arrived.

It was late morning by the time the nuns and the girls left. They didn't get to see the rest of the retreat center sink to its knees in ashes. Instead they got to ride in a milk truck, with chains fastened all around its tires like loose-fitting fishnet stockings or charm bracelets. The rain and the snow, having divided the day between them, had united at last in ice, which was thickly coating every twig, every fussy little branchlet, with its own diamond shell. The girls were entranced. To Alice it seemed like God's spit, hardening, jeweling everything; cracking everything too, if the predictions of the milk-truck driver were to be believed. "Keeps on like this, it'll be known as the ice blizzard of 1968," he bellowed as he tucked blankets around them. "Trees'll be down from here to the Canadian border. You girls'll tell this all to your grandchildren. How're you good sisters, nice and toasty now?"

"So kind," the nuns agreed. "These poor things, a terrible shock." They tended to bleat when confronted with men who did things like drive trucks. Sister John Bosco, however, looked out over the fields and didn't say anything. She held Sister Vincent de Paul's hands between hers, very tightly, and her lips moved with words Alice couldn't hear.

The road shone like cellophane. Once the milk truck skidded, and they all screamed as if they were on the fourteen-foot roller coaster at the Sacred Heart June fair. Alice sat as near Sister Vincent de Paul as she could, though it was Sister John Boss's job to carry the worry.

In such dilemmas as this it was important, the nuns knew, to get onto the regular schedule as soon as possible. So the next morning, back home in their usual red brick convent school on Fifth Avenue in Troy, New York, Sister

John Bosco called Alice Colossus for an interview before morning classes. Things such as fires and ice storms never occurred here at home, and Alice, like her companions, was sorry to be home.

"Have you thought anymore about the Harrigans?" said Sister John Bosco. "I have promised them an answer by the end of the week."

"How is Sister Vincent de Paul?" said Alice.

"You must roll your tongue if you are to be understood, Alice. We're all very tired of reminding you." Sister John Bosco did not mean to be cruel, and Alice understood this. It had been a trying weekend. The girls had been on their best behavior, but the retreat center had burned down anyway. It must be hard for Sister John Bosco to keep going.

"How is burned Sister?" Alice tried again, with a great exercising of muscles and a sarcastic lacing of spittle to show her effort. "Don't she get to come home, too?"

"She is at rest in the hospital," said Sister John Boss, warily. The blank look, to protect the young from sadness, rose in her face. "Sister Vincent de Paul is well provided for. Classes begin shortly, Alice. You were to be deciding this weekend. The Harrigans are very kind to be considering adopting you. They are good people and won't be put off by your defects. Have you given it much thought?"

Alice Colossus munched her inner lip. The snow, glorious and dangerous and white up north, had fallen gray and smudgy here, or so you'd think peering out through Sister John Boss's double casement window. What had Sister Vincent de Paul been saying when the fire broke out? She had pointed up to the roof with her spoon. She had said that a cold front and a warm front had met right overhead. Perhaps God and the devil had stood just over the house, in heaven, their toes touching while they stood seething at each other. Perhaps they were waiting to see what decision Alice would make about the Harrigans. They were hissing mad. It was rain on one side and snow on the other. But which was which? And how could you make the right choice? And while you were deciding, fire down below, the ordinary worldly kind, could engulf you.

"Alice," rapped Sister John Bosco. "You're drifting again. Don't freeze me out, Alice; I've no time this morning."

Alice dug her fingers into the waistband of her uniform skirt. She flexed her tongue. She breathed very shallowly and was conscious of the rise and fall of her breastbone against the top fluttery edge of the garment Sister Jake called a camisole and the girls called a tit-bit. From the corridors came the clamor of the first bell. A laden silence, then shrieking: girls being let loose from the dormitory wing to flood forward into the day school. The chatter drowned out whatever clarity of thought Alice had. It was with a certain relief that she answered Sister John Bosco.

"When Sister Vincent de Paul comes back," she said, "I'll decide then." By the opening of Sister John Bosco's exhausted mouth, to protest or forbid, Alice saw that she had been heard very clearly, and understood.

MY FAIR LADY

Alice had made a secret bargain with God. A holy contract. Make Sister Vincent de Paul not die, and then I will think about the Harrigans. I can't care about everybody in the world at once; I'm not like You: I have a smallish heart. *And* I'm stubborn, Alice reminded God. The nuns all say so, and You should know it by now.

But in return God was testing Alice's nerve. On the one hand, Sister Vincent de Paul, who didn't return to the Sacred Heart Home for Girls. On the other, the Harrigans. For fifteen years they had waited; neither God's grace nor the luck of the Irish had allowed Mrs. Harrigan to get pregnant. They'd swallowed their pride at last and gone to the orphanage, but they weren't in a mood to hang around now.

Sister John Bosco refused their request to see Alice.

They wanted to explain why they couldn't stand the suspense and were moving ahead with Plan B. "Cut it clean, it's kindest, I won't have it otherwise," the nun declared. But Alice happened to be on her way to singing practice—hah! that she could sing and also hah! that her route took her through the front hall—and she just happened to pass the parlor as the Harrigans were leaving.

"Look, it's little Alice," said Mr. Harrigan, not meanly. He was hardly taller than Alice, and she flinched to be reminded of her gangly limbs. Mrs. Harrigan smiled. She was a nut case, Alice decided. Her hair was an ad for Breck; her whole head looked sprayed and polished like a chestnut bowling ball. Her breasts really filled out that Maidenform bra, Alice thought a little coolly, a little jealously. "I knew I'd see you again," Mrs. Harrigan gushed at Alice. She wore gloves and a pleated skirt, and in a furry circlet around her neck a fox bit its own tail. To keep from laughing out loud at its owner? wondered Alice. "Alice," moaned Mrs. Harrigan, "Alice, we'd have you if you'd have us. Oh, Moss, I feel so awful. But we can't wait. Oh, Moss, whoever knew motherhood would be so hard?"

"Steady on, Eileen, it hasn't begun yet," said Mr. Moss Harrigan. "It's the girl's choice, and we come second. Fair enough." But he grinned at Alice as if he knew his wife was really loopy.

"Alice, move along to where you're expected," said Sister John Boss in a voice like tarnish.

"I'm sorry, Mr. and Mrs. Harrigan," said Alice. She tried to think about the weight of God and Satan in the heavens, and Sister Vincent de Paul getting hurt while the sky hung on hinges above, but could only mutter, "Sorry, I mean very very," and scurry along.

"We could've come to understand her. I was *good* at languages in high school," said Mrs. Harrigan to Sister John Boss. "Maybe we just never got through to her."

"Alice is working on her own agenda, at her own pace," said the nun soothingly, then more things Alice couldn't hear. Her last sight of the Harrigans was in the tall, black-flecked mirror as they clucked and bowed to Sister John Bosco. What's one way of life next to another? thought Alice. I could have gone away with them and loved it, or hated it. At least here I know what I'm up against.

Still, she felt cheated. It was certainly within almighty God's almighty godliness to have restored Sister Vincent de Paul in time. Sure, Alice might still have chosen *against* the Harrigans, but at least it'd have been her real choice. God knew she was sacrificing for Sister Vincent de Paul, bribing Him so that the burned nun would get better. Alice didn't care. If a bribe worked, it worked.

Only it wasn't working yet. She had to suffer some more for God to relent and be merciful as everyone insisted He was. Sister Vincent de Paul, for all she knew, was no more than a lumpy corpse in a glass coffin at some side altar somewhere. Waxy cheeks and folded fingers. A new veil to cover the bubbled scalp, the huge shoe done up with a fine flourish of its laces. Maybe even studded in the heel and toe with taps, as the girls had always promised themselves they'd do for her. And outside the walls of the coffin, where the world still wriggled on, beeswax candles making that stiff, hot smell in the cold, stone-squeezed

17

air. A few wildflowers in a jelly jar. But who was there to mourn Sister Vincent de Paul?

The good sisters of Mind Your Own Sweet Business wouldn't answer Alice's questions directly. "She's safely at rest," they'd say. "She's resting comfortably." What a crock! For one thing Sister Vincent de Paul *never*, but never rested, comfortably or otherwise. Grimace though she might at the strain to her joints brought on by her bad foot, she was an up-and-at-'em creature. If she was really *resting*, she wouldn't be *resting*; she'd be twisting in the bed, clanging a spoon against the metal don't-fall-out rails, knitting with her IV tubes out of boredom, boredom, boredom. "I have no mind," she used to say in the kitchen. "God said I could either live on the street like a tramp, or cook in a convent. Not for me the classroom or the hospital! Wrong kind of bedside manner for a nurse, and no brain to back it up! No brain to deal with the kids! So I chose. Do I mind? Do I mind my choice? Alice?"

"Do you mind your choice?" asked Alice.

"Not mo-yound. *Mind*. Do I mind giving up the hot-cha-cha?"

"Do you miiiiind giving up the hotchy-chotchy?"

"No I do not!" A thump of fist into a tired pillow of bread dough. "Not in the least! Don't mind the choices, Alice; mind the details! The smell of this bread! Here! Stick your nose in it! Right into it!" She'd demonstrated, coming up gluey and smelling raw as ripped, wet brown paper. "Mind the moments, Alice, and the choices don't make a whit of difference."

But you *like* to cook, Alice wanted to point out. With

18

her face plunged into dough, however, the time to make that remark came and went.

And what choice might Sister Vincent de Paul have had in resting comfortably? Or was that term just nuns' hand-lotion niceness, like the Final Slumber, the Bus Ride Home to Jesus, the Great Convent in the Sky, the Eternal Sleep of the Just? Sister Vincent de Paul's room hadn't been cleared out; that was some consolation. While delivering linen to the wardrobe outside the sisters' wing, Alice had stolen for a moment into forbidden territory. Sister Vincent de Paul had a Snoopy cutout on the inside of her door that Alice had made her last Christmas. And there was the door, open, Snoopy taped on it still. Inside: a veil on a hook, a tidily made bed, a bottle of Geritol on the windowsill. Not so much as a tendril of dust. They hadn't taken down the Snoopy; that was all the proof Alice needed that, platitudes aside, Sister Vincent de Paul was still somewhere in the land of the living.

Staring for a minute at the brown linoleum floor, waxed so thick as to look an inch deep in water, Alice stood on her upside downness. If Sister Vincent de Paul was out there languishing, she would by Christ (a prayer, not a swear) bring her home through her own good works and elevation of spirit.

"Alice, you're dawdling," observed Sister John Boss from across the brown lake of the front hall. Alice leaped over to the stairs, stepping adroitly on her reflection's soles.

This was Saturday, when the daily rules were somewhat loosened. Things were meant to be fun. And often they were. Today, for instance, some of the girls were going to practice their parts for a student production of the musical comedy *My Fair Lady*.

The story was a delicious one. (The whole school had gone to see the movie, which they loved because for once it wasn't a Bible movie.) It was about a poor, young flower girl, Eliza Doolittle, who couldn't speak well to save her life. She sang pretty well, though, and a man who taught speaking lessons met her. He sort of fell in love with her, although the student production wasn't emphasizing that part very much. He taught her to speak like a queen, however, and then she got to wear fancy clothes and go to parties. She was beautiful, like the Ugly Duckling all grown up. The girls of Sacred Heart were doing the female roles, and the boys of Saint Mary's across the river in Albany were learning the male roles.

Alice, to everyone's surprise, including her own, had been chosen to play Eliza Doolittle. Alice's speech problems gave her a convincing advantage in the part. But because it was such a long show, Alice only played Eliza up till Eliza learned to speak clearly. Then Naomi Matthews played perfect-tongued Eliza through the end of the play.

Sister Isaac Jogues was waiting in the rec room. The wreck room. The other girls were annoyed and showing it when Alice arrived, late. She hadn't known they'd all be there. She had hoped this would be a strictly solo rehearsal. "Sorry," she panted.

"Not sow-oww-wee, Alice," said Sister Ike.

"Not celery, Alice," said Rebecca Luke.

"Can it, Rebecca, or I'll can you," said Sister Ike. Rebecca made a face and popped her gum defiantly. Gum was allowed in the wreck room, but it still seemed disobedient and fun to flaunt it, especially when a nun was there.

Rebecca Luke, Sarah Corinth, and Naomi the-queen-of-the-hive Matthews. Alice had looked forward to being alone with Sister Ike and maybe pumping her about Sister Vincent de Paul. But the wreck room was now a zoo for prima donnas. They made Alice sick. Only after a minute did she notice little Ruth Peters, thumb jammed in her gooey mouth as usual, lying on the battered sofa and kicking at the pillows. Alice's self-pity lightened up. Tough it out, she told herself. Kick out like Ruth. You can learn something from a four-year-old.

"All right, this'll be noisy but I don't know how else to manage it." Sister Ike took over. "Naomi, put the record on low. Practice that 'I Could Have Danced All Night' section, where the chorus parts come in. It's notes you're after, not volume. Can you do that?"

"Alice can't hear; she won't be bothered," said Naomi. "We can be loud."

"I can too hear," said Alice.

"Oh, sow-oww-wee, forgive me." Naomi flounced away. Her star role was definitely going to her head. "Come on, Sarah and Rebecca. Let's do this right." The three intergalactic comets flowed away to the other side of the room. Alice noticed she and Sister Ike were suddenly in the empty half of the room.

"Now Alice, your part is just as important. I hope you understand this," said Sister Ike. She thumped out a C major chord to bring Alice in. "The show won't work unless your character works. We're all *very* pleased you are taking part. It shows real team spirit. And this is such a nice show."

Across the room the record revolved steadily, thirty-three revolutions per minute. Julie Andrews from the turntable and Naomi Matthews in the flesh pealed in a duet. Julie Andrews sang with notes coated in ice, like the trees two weeks ago when the snow and rain joined up. You could see and hear through her words clear to the other side. Transparencies. Even Alice could. Naomi Matthews, in Alice's humble opinion, sounded like slush. When the violins and flutes arabesqued up to a jittery pinnacle, Naomi's voice declared Eliza-the-character's love of dancing by going shrill and high, all out of pitch, loud as a police siren.

Ruth Peters reared herself up on the sofa and said loudly, "She *can too* hear." So they piped down a bit and adjusted the volume, though Naomi continued to make broad gestures of how she would dance in her white night-gown and sing with perfect diction, throwing her arms out like this, like this, like this. If that's what I'm going to be like when I improve my speaking, thought Alice, forget it. I'd rather mumble.

"*Alice.*" Sister Ike knocked her fist against Alice's surprised forehead. "Hello in there. I'm playing the intro, and you're supposed to be listening."

Sister Ike cascaded her fingers again in a little Highland fling across the keys. Alice attended. She opened her mouth and sang when the time seemed right. The song was a listing of everything that would make Eliza happy.

Alice wasn't very strong on remembering words. "What I'd like blah blah blah some-time. Can't re-mem-ber the rest some-time, blah blah blah—"

"Words, Alice," sang Sister Ike, mouthing them exaggeratedly so Alice could read her lips.

"And life would be so heavenly!" She always remembered that line. The real song said it a different way, but the nuns didn't approve of the word *loverly* around the home. It was Alice's favorite line and she gave it gusto. Ruth Peters applauded. Naomi had turned her back, and her shoulders were shaking. There were twisted, bitten little smiles on Rebecca's and Sarah's faces.

"I can't do this!" cried Alice.

Sister Ike went plowing on with the next verse.

"And life would be so heavenly!" sang Alice grimly. "Heavenly! Heavenly! Heavenly! Heavenly!"

It wasn't very heavenly, but that apparently was why they were practicing. They went over it six, eight, ten times, till even Ruth Peters was mouthing the words Alice couldn't remember. Naomi meanwhile Rained in Spain. She practiced being Eliza Doolittle at the ball, flouncing out her imaginary gown as if dogs were nosing naughtily up at her and she had to shoo them away with little backhanded motions. Finally Sister John Bosco called for her over the PA and she left, her bodyguards bobbing along behind her. Little Ruth Peters quietly wet the sofa rather than get up and leave Sister Isaac Jogues and Alice. Ruth was sort of in love with Alice.

Sister Ike kept gamely on for some time. Finally she sighed, though, and closed the lid of the piano. "Look at the time. Alice, I guess you'd better go downstairs and give this sheet music to Father Laverty. He's driving over to Saint Mary's in Albany to say Mass for the boys this afternoon. He can deliver the music to Brother Antoine. Give him this envelope with cash in it, too. It's the money we owe him for the record album." Brother Antoine over there was the director of the boys' roles. He'd be training Professor Higgins and Eliza's father and the boyfriend, Freddy. Sacred Heart and Saint Mary's would never be ready to put on this joint production in a month, of course. It was doomed to failure. Alice didn't even know why she was wasting her time.

"Yes, Sister," she said, and went downstairs.

The hall was empty. Most of the girls had gone for a Saturday matinee of some boring Walt Disney comedy with dogs and kids in it. Sister Francis de Sales was the only one around on the first floor. She was transcribing notes from a taped lecture and removed her headphones only when Alice made signs of *please*. If everyone could lip-read as well as *she* could, Alice thought smugly, the world would run very smoothly.

"What is it, Alice?"

"Father Laverty?"

"Father Laverty? Is that what you're trying to say? He just left. You might catch him in the parking lot if you hurry."

Alice hurried. The side door slammed behind her. Father Laverty's little Volkswagen beetle was parked there. He must still be inside. Maybe he'd been in the men's room on the first floor. He was the only one who ever used it. Alice often wondered who cleaned it, if anyone. Nuns were too sensitive even to think about a men's room, but there it was.

Music and cash envelope in hand, Alice headed back to the side door. But, with Saturday security measures, it had locked behind her. She picked her way through the snow mush in the parking lot around to the front door. No one answered the bell. Well, Sister Frank had the headphones on, of course. And the girls weren't allowed to answer the door. . . . Besides, they'd probably all left for the movie theater. Where had Sister Isaac Jogues gone? Maybe she was running a bath to wash Ruth Peters.

Alice rang and rang, beginning to feel the cold. She had on an oversized blue cardigan, a nun's reject sweater, which hung like a tunic over her hips, but even so. The air bullied her into shivering. Then she remembered the kitchen door and had gone around another corner of the building and down the unshoveled steps before she realized—yes—the steps were unshoveled because Sister Vincent de Paul was gone. Sister Vincent de Paul wasn't there. Through the window of the locked door, the kitchen looked cold and dark, and the blue pilot lights were like squat vigil candles in their cast-iron cage. It was send-out-to-Neba's-for-submarine-sandwiches for sure tonight.

Maybe Father Laverty had a key. She'd wait by his car for him to come out. But when she ran around again to the parking lot, the little rusty heap of Volkswagen was gone.

Gone! And without the music for the boys at Saint Mary's!

Now Alice was in trouble for being outside the school

without permission—Sister Frank's bored directions wouldn't stand up as approval. Alice knew this from experience. And she would get yelled at, also, for going outside without her coat in February. And for not completing the task assigned her—to deliver the music and money to Father Laverty. As if everyone wasn't already cross at her for stalling the Harrigans, for annoying and disappointing them.

How hard it is to be good, Alice thought as she began to stride down the street away from the school. She didn't hope for the fame of sainthood as Naomi Matthews did. She just wanted to tiptoe around the occasions of terrible sin, if she could manage it. Yet the world kept shuffling itself in ways that shoved her forward in the wrong directions. Like being spun through a revolving door and falling into the wrong company on the other side. "You're not bad, Alice," Sister John Bosco would say. "Not a bad girl in any instance. Not bad behavior. But unfortunate. At times unthinking. Were you thinking?"

She *was* thinking! She was always thinking! As she caught the bus for downtown, paying with some change from the money envelope, Alice thought: I'm always at work in my brain. I just am thinking about the other side of things, not the way nuns think.

Troy seemed today like a city built out of sand or salt, half dissolved in the opposing forces of weather. The red brick factories and mills; the brownstone town houses; the formal buildings of Russell Sage College all pulled away from the sidewalks as if fearful of catching something from their unsavory neighbors. The whole city wobbled on the edge of the great steel Hudson River and threatened to go lurching in. Or maybe it was the sleet starting to fall that gave it that look. I love Troy, thought Alice. Hideous place. I wonder if Sister Vincent de Paul misses it? Or is she in a hospital here somewhere?

On one of her regular visits to the ear doctors, Alice had seen a Capital District bus marked for Albany parked across the street from the clinic. And—a miracle—*there one was*, exhaust puffing out the tail pipe, magic accordion door open, driver waiting, reading the *Times Union*. A bus to Albany was a very *minor* miracle; Alice realized this. But it did seem like a sign that she was doing the right thing. And when she didn't have the correct change from the cash envelope and a young man carrying a guitar in a duffle bag made up the difference, Alice felt positively anointed.

Albany was what, eight, ten miles away? Four? It was across the river, she knew that. Saint Christopher, patron saint of travelers, who carried the Christ Child piggyback across the river, save me from drowning in case the bus plunges off the Dunn Memorial Bridge. Or whatever bridge we use. Amen.

The smell of diesel oil in the bus was quite strong.

Alice hoped she wasn't misbehaving. She wasn't always clear in her mind about it. She had to be good, so that Christ would ladle forgiveness out of His bottomless bucket o' mercy. She was doing the job Sister Frank had given her, so that Sister Vincent de Paul would recover and come home. It only *looked* like she was running away.

"Without Satan, that snake, we'd never have needed

the love of Christ," Sister Vincent de Paul was fond of saying. "So we should thank Satan kindly for tempting Adam and Eve. Because of their stupidity we got to get Jesus in our world." Alice hadn't quite been able to follow this, but cut her thoughts off early. God was hard to figure out; Jesus and Mary were much chummier and Alice preferred them. But God was the boss God, and Alice tried not to be disrespectful.

From bad mistakes, from accidents and disasters, good could grow. This is what Alice wanted to believe.

The young man—well, he was a boy—the one with the guitar, he was changing his seat. "Mind if I sit here?"

Alice nodded yes, then shook her head no, then gestured: Sit.

She had to grin a few minutes later. He didn't realize she was a clumsy talker. He yakked so much all she had to do was nod or shrug. When he put his arm around her, however, she said as distinctly as she could, "Stop it, please." She might be tall, but she sure wasn't old enough for this kind of nonsense.

"You just looked cold, no coat and all," he said.

She nodded—yes she was cold—and yes—she still meant what she said. Then she removed his hand with hers and said with inspiration (Holy Ghost sanctify me, Holy Ghost enlighten me): "Play your guitar instead."

"Play my cigar?" But he wasn't being mean. He got it from the bag; its neck stuck out in the aisle. "What'll I play, tootsie? Beatles?"

Alice made a face. "Play *My Fair Lady*." Wasn't he a fair one himself, though, with those soft brown curls?

He laughed again. "Okay, *My Fair Lady*, my fair lady. Which song?"

"It don't matter." She thought some more. "Heavenly one."

After a while he figured it out. He even sang, too, a kind of nice voice in a cold city bus. The snow that people had tracked in was melting in rivulets down the grooved wooden floor of the bus. Below them, below the bridge, skaters circled on the gray marble slab of river. The sky had strange blotchy yellow-brown clouds in it, like butter streaked on wax paper.

Alice joined in on the lines she could remember. The sleet came down, but with the noise of windshield wipers and music she couldn't hear it. Other passengers, even the driver, began to sing. When they finished, they started all over. Alice let her voice out like a fishing line in a pool, a little at a time, letting it get louder, unreeling it. Nobody laughed the way Naomi and her friends had.

All too soon the château on the top of State Street in Albany showed up, red pointy roofs almost pewter-colored under the sleet. "That's our State Capitol building," said the guy. "My name's—" Alice didn't quite catch it, and didn't want to. "I'm taking the Pine Hills bus back to the state college dorms. Want to come along?"

A college boy!

Alice blushed. She was hip-deep in trouble now. With some effort she managed to say that she needed to find Saint Mary's School for Boys. The orphans-and-trouble-makers school—did he know it? He did. It was even on the same city-bus route. He would take her there.

"I can't go to your college," she said forcefully, so he wouldn't be expecting things.

"I'm cool," he said. "Doesn't matter. I'll still show you where you're going."

And so he did, although as the next bus crawled along the streets and Alice noticed cars switching on their headlights, she began to feel that she was getting quite a bit farther from the parking lot of the Sacred Heart Home for Girls than she'd intended. Is that how Eve swallowed the apple too—she was just thinking of something else, and bang, there it was with a big, white, tooth-marked, mouth-shaped cave in it, in her hand, and the juice running down her chin for the rest of her short sorry life?

Is there a dotted line beyond which the apostles and angels won't help you anymore? Peg you as a loser? Cut their losses and turn their attentions to a more docile soul, a likelier prospect for the company of saints? If you belonged in Troy, did that dotted line in your case run through, say, downtown Albany? Should she throw herself off the bus and wheel wildly around in the other direction? It was even getting dark. She had no coat.

She stayed on the bus.

On they churned through the slush. Each city block seemed to Alice as dense and infinite as a state of the union. She would never get home. What had she been thinking of? Girls from the Sacred Heart weren't allowed to go out alone! Even the nuns traveled in pairs, and only with permission of Sister John Bosco! The bus flew westward, away from Troy and Albany, in a matter of minutes crossing the borders of Ohio, Indiana, Illinois, Wyoming in her imagination.

"Here's our stop," said the guitar boy, and pulled a cord that made no sound Alice could catch—but the bus stopped and out they tumbled.

"Thank you," said Alice to her savior and persecutor. He grinned, and they fell into step together on icy, slate paving stones, under elms, next to snow-covered yards that seemed to Alice as wide as prairies and the lonesome range where the deer and the antelope play. The streetlights came on, one at a time, as if being plugged in by a man in a basement in the State Capitol.

"Here's Saint Mary's," said the college kid. "Can I come in?"

"No," said Alice, and ran up the walk. "Sorry," she flung over her shoulder, hoping he understood it. "Sorry. Bye." She pressed the bell marked OUT OF ORDER—PLEASE USE KNOCKER. She pressed it again. She knocked out of desperation, not understanding. He stood in the sleet, not going away, in a cone of streetlight, traffic making a blurred pattern of noise and light behind him.

The door at last opened. There were three boys in sweaters. A receptionist—a Franciscan in sandals and thick, hairy socks—was getting up from behind the desk, putting down his paperback of *The Valley of the Dolls*. Alice whirled around and cried out to her friend—

"Heavenly!"

She was back home within the hour. Father Laverty had understood her predicament without picking too hard at the reasoning. "You're a good girl, Alice," he'd said, putting his coat around her and shoveling her into his car. "You're a good girl." He was trying to convince her. She wasn't convinced.

31

"You delivered the music. Good for you. You didn't get permission to leave. And you wouldn't have. But you didn't mean to disobey, I'm sure." Father Laverty was too good. He behaved as if you were better than you were. But Alice felt bullied into accepting his kindness. She had actually liked sitting with the college boy. Sort of. In a friendly way.

"Tell you what we'll do," said Father Laverty, guiding his little car through neighborhoods made mysterious by the black winter night and the white snow falling against it. "I've got a key to Sacred Heart. I'll unlock the side door and see if you can slip in. If there's no hubbub, all the better. But don't lie about it if anyone has noticed you were missing. Tell the truth and tell Sister John Boss to call me if she needs proof."

Sister John Boss. He called her that, too. Alice looked at him sideways. He winked at her. "And do this again, Alice Colossus, and you're in very hot water."

"I took some money for the bus," she told him, to get it all over with.

"We'll let it go this time," he said.

She relaxed. He smelled like cigarettes and mothballs and sweat. He was a big, fat young man, pinker than nuns, with huge bare hands like Mickey Mouse gloves. "Do you know where Sister Vincent de Paul is staying, is she getting okay?" she said.

"You're very attached to Sister Vincent de Paul," he observed. She realized he hadn't exactly understood her question. But he went on. "I heard about that couple who wanted to take you in on a trial basis. The Harrisons?"

"Harrigans," she said, and even to her it sounded like Hooligans.

"I wish you'd given them a chance," he said. "You're a likable young person. But Sister Vincent de Paul's accident has stood in the way. You must move on, Alice. As Jesus said—"

He paused for so long that even Alice knew Jesus had never uttered a word about orphans abandoning their good friends who happened to be nuns.

"As Jesus said," he continued, pulling up in front of the home, "it ain't over till it's over." He grinned at her. "Be good. And better leave my coat here—they'll wonder."

She nodded her thanks. Under his big, fat, unthreatening arm she was hustled to the side door. "Say your prayers," he said, rolling his eyes at the idea of anxious sisters inside. "I'm getting outta here while the getting's good."

"Right," she said, and slipped away inside.

Safely, as it turned out. She'd reached the second-floor stairs before anyone saw her. "Oh, there you are. We're taking orders for subs," said Sister John Vianney. "Roast beef or tuna?"

"Tuna," said Alice, mainly because it was easier to say.

In the lavatory she rinsed her face. Her shoulder felt warm. She pulled back her cardigan and blouse to see the pale knob of shoulder. It was not red. It was not warm from Father Laverty but from the young man with the guitar. The warmth dried the snow from her hair and the fear from her throat. She was only twelve. She remembered this and thought about it.

Naomi Matthews came rushing in. "Oh, Alice," she said, all brightness, an Up with People medley all by herself. She must be back to being holy again after her nastiness earlier. She began to brush her terracotta hair as if beating a rug, fiercely, out of joy. "You'll never guess. Sister John Bosco, she called me from the wreck room? Remember? It was those Harrigans. They were so upset by seeing you again today, they wanted to take another chance. They talked to me. They're going to see about taking *me!* I just told them one thing. If they said yes they wanted me, then I'd do it. I'd give it a try. But I just couldn't go until after *My Fair Lady*. It wouldn't be fair. I couldn't leave you in the lurch like that."

The two Eliza Doolittles stared at each other in the bathroom mirror. Behind them the radiators clanked and cleared their throats. The bad Eliza, who couldn't speak English correctly, just kept feeling her shoulder. The good Eliza, who would come on stage after the character had learned to speak correctly and be beautiful and sophisticated and rich, rubbed her hands through the static of her maniacal hair. "I just knew you'd be thrilled," said Naomi Matthews. "I just hoped I'd be the one to tell you."

Naomi then bowed to herself in the mirror, accepting applause; she hurried to the door and bowed to Alice. Alice and her reflection bowed back. She bowed again after Naomi had gone, until her forehead touched the cold porcelain of the sink. She rested her face in its cold, white cave, nesting in its echoes, like Eve being surrounded by the apple's white cave, Eve being deafened by the echoes of her deed.

Part Two
KINGDOM COME

By common agreement Miami's birthday was April sixth. Since Christmas she'd been coaxing and whining to be allowed to wear rhinestone earrings on that special day. The party was going to be *big*, she announced. It was going to be *loud*, like an eighth grader's graduation party, although Miami was only twelve and still—and barely— in fifth grade. It was going to have boys. No it wasn't, boys stank. Well, maybe it was. She'd see. Both possibilities were examined thoroughly by a panel of fifth-grade experts at recess every day. At home, the discussion was clipped.

"Your party can have boys," said Garth, who was five and didn't like Miami's girlfriends.

"What's the dif," said Miami. "*You're* not coming to it."

"Why not? Where's it gonna be?" said Garth.

"Wherever you're not," said Miami.

"I don't get it," said Garth. "I'm not not."

Miami leaned her face close to her brother's. "You're a little accident. Do my party a favor and banana split."

"Mom!" yelled Garth, from lungs that seemed to fill 90 percent of his small frame. He was unruffled and precise in his announcement. "Miami called me a little accident again."

Mrs. Shaw made a loud noise in the kitchen. By the time she appeared at the doorway she was quite calm. "Miami, did you say something to your little brother?"

"I *said*," said Miami, working her jaw like a slide trombone, "I *said* it was an accident he was a boy and couldn't come to my party."

"He'll be at your party no matter what you decide, darling. He lives here. So do we. You can choose your friends, but you can't choose your family. They're with you for the long haul."

"*That's* a laugh," snorted Miami. "You can't choose your family? *I'm not being rude*"—she knew what her mother would say—"I'm just pointing out that *you* chose four children to adopt. It's a fact."

But Mrs. Shaw just laughed. "I walked right into that one," she said. "Of course there's choice, sometimes. But there are rules, too, honey. A family is a commune. We all work together for the good of—"

"A *commune*?" Miami played at being scandalized. "Are you turning into some kind of hippie in an apron? We better get the social worker in here, pronto. I've never been so shocked in all my born days." She pretended to be shocked over the tops of imaginary eyeglasses, like an old prude.

"A commune is a perfectly good English word, and it applies to families, too," said Mrs. Shaw. She sat down on the hassock with an unopened bag of frozen peas in her hands, and as she talked she worked her hands over the solid mass, separating them. It looked like calming work, and Miami wouldn't have minded trying. But Garth meandered over and put his big old head in his mother's lap.

"I hope," said Miami, with as much dignity as she could muster, "I most sincerely hope I'm not in for lecture number one hundred and fourteen: How Being a Negro Is Just As Good As Being Anyone Else. I already agree. Garth's problem isn't that he's black. It's that he's a boy."

"Hee hee hee," squealed Garth into the peas. Mrs. Shaw was tickling him.

"I *was* revving up," admitted Mrs. Shaw. "Now I'm all warmed up and have no place to go. How about number seventy-five?"

"What's that?"

"How you're the oldest and have to set a good example."

"*Bor*-ing."

"Well, honey, it's true. Now that you're twelve—"

"She's still eleven-going-on-twelve!" said Garth. "Until Saturday when there's a party. I get to go to it, too!"

"You want my opinion?" said Miami conversationally. "This family is crazy. Two crazy parents, one perfectly

37

sane preteen, one crazy brother, and two crazy baby sisters whose names sound like diaper rash!"

"Miami!"

"Well they *do*! Nobody has a baby named *Fanny*! Fanny and Rachelle! Fanny rash!"

As if they had heard their names, the girls woke up from their afternoon nap and began to wail. "Now, Miami, that's just enough of that," said Mrs. Shaw. "Fun is fun, but I won't have you picking on your brother and sisters. Frances was my grandmother's name, and Fanny was a common nickname years ago. Fanny can choose to be Franny or Fran when she grows up. If she wants."

Miami murmured something rude under her breath.

"What is *eating* you?" said Mrs. Shaw. "Are you worried no boys will come to your party?"

"Of *course* not!" shouted Miami. "I can't stand here and talk nonsense all day!" She shot out of the living room and up the stairs to the tower.

But of course that was it. What if no boys came? What if they thought she was just a stupid girl? If she had to have one more party with just girlfriends she'd scream.

It was a relief to have the tower. Mrs. Shaw called it the Alone Room. Mr. Shaw called it Shaw's Folly. Garth wasn't allowed up in it. Fanny and Rachelle were too young to know about it. So Miami swam through the dusty shadows of the main attic, past skis and cardboard cartons of Christmas decorations and a couple of strap-bound steamer trunks, to the ladder that led to the tower. Each time, she put her foot on the bottom rung and tested. There was a screech of rusty nail against a stubborn old board somewhere. She imagined the ladder coming loose, as if a knight on a castle battlement above were pushing the ladder away from the castle walls. But each time it held. She emerged into the cool octagonal area as if climbing out of a pool—or a moat.

Eight small windows. One of them could be jostled open. Miami hadn't yet had the nerve to climb out onto the roof. It was so high. She would bounce, how many times, if she slipped and fell? On the sloping roof, tiled in chipped slate; on the front porch roof; on the small, level front yard where Garth had his baby wading pool all summer; on the long overgrown slope down to South Allen Street. Four times. She'd be dead as JFK by the time she came to a rest.

She leaned on the windowsill. The trees were still bare, and the square top of Saint Peter's Hospital could still be seen all those blocks away. From here you could see the street was streaked with the runoff of last week's snowfall. She imagined the fuss if she fell. Mrs. Shaw running out on the porch. Is that—it can't be! *Oh my God* . . . Her hand put tremblingly up to a quivering mouth. Garth trailing along like the leech he was. Don't look, it's too, too horrible, darling! Maybe she wouldn't be dead yet. Mr. Shaw could be walking over the hill from where the bus dropped him off on Western Avenue. Oh, sweet Jesus— it's my baby— He would run, long, slow-motion strides, his London Fog belted raincoat flapping open. His briefcase would be flung aside. With any luck it would smack old crabby next-door neighbor Mrs. Jenkins on the noggin and good-bye Jenkins. He would get to his daughter's neat, oddly bloodless near-corpse just as Mrs. Shaw arrived, scrambling down the wooden steps to the street level. They'd be sorry they hadn't had those steps painted last fall when they showed up on the news on channels six, ten, and thirteen. News crews would just happen to be coming along South Allen Street. Here'd be a great story! An innocent little adopted girl, fallen to her pretty death from a height of—she fell from way up there? The cameras would pan to emphasize the horror of it. That *ledge* on the tower at the *top* of that tall house? And then down that steep slope through the brambles and the litter that collected there no matter how often the little angel had been assigned to clear it away?

Little darling! Speak into the microphone.

Please . . . my last wish . . . Her voice would carry with such a vibrato even hard-boiled newsmen would tear up. Invite my friends to what would've been my twelfth birthday party anyway. No yucky boys. But if Billy O'Hara insists on coming . . . And please . . . Mama? Papa? Bury me . . .

Bury me . . .

(Everyone strains forward to catch this last bit.)

. . . with rhinestone earrings . . .

Her head would loll, her eyelids flutter down. Garth would pitch himself on her body and beg forgiveness for being such a pain in the neck.

And then, thought Miami with a gentle, pale smile, I'll come back and haunt the whole lot of them from here to kingdom come.

The night was rippling in, on faint breezes like an airy

tide. Miami loved being in the tower when evening arrived. The air was purple with a hint of green, as if the trees were thinking of flowering. She could see Mrs. Jenkins down below, scraping the ground with a bristly rake. That woman would come out and iron the snow in her yard, just about. She was just so obsessed with neatness. If Garth or Miami so much as accidentally breathed in the smell of her lilacs, or worse yet, let a ball bounce into her yard, she was out on the porch in moccasins and a housecoat having a heart attack in public. She straightened the grass blade by blade, and resurrected it with Dippity-Do hair styling gel. Just about. Miami couldn't understand nuts like Mrs. Jenkins.

There was Garth. It was April, and he was still wearing snow pants, those fat, squeaky things. He wandered around the yard looking for something to play with. He was bored because dinner was even later than usual; Mr. Shaw hadn't come home yet. It was too dark to find ants to kill, which was Garth's hobby last summer. He was going to be an exterminator when he grew up, Mr. Shaw said. He should practice on old Hag Nag Jenkins.

He didn't know she was there. His voice spiraled up to Miami. She leaned a bit farther out to try to hear what he was saying.

"Hi, Mrs. Jenkins," said Garth in his fluting, small-boy's voice.

What an Eddie Haskell. Garth didn't like Jenkins any more than she did. Or maybe he was too young to keep his dislikes constant in his mind.

Mrs. Jenkins was walking to the fence. She was leaning

over. Miami watched carefully. Garth annoyed her, but she didn't want to see him kidnapped or anything. Mrs. Jenkins had a cooey-dovey voice that was hard to pick up from this far away.

"What king?" said Garth loudly.

A fluttery explanation. Who did she think she was talking to? Garth had the brains of a bowl of soggy Cheerios.

"Oooh!" said Garth. "I better tell my mom! Bye, Mrs. Jenkins!" He waddled away. Mrs. Jenkins stood with her rake in her hand, still. She came back to her senses in a minute, though, and began flinging a wheelbarrow around her yard, pelting the soil with handfuls of lime.

Another notch of dark. Lights came on across the street. Other families were finishing their dinners, and kids were starting on their homework. The Shaws ate late, waiting for Mr. Shaw. High as she was, Miami couldn't quite see down into West Lawrence Street, where the O'Haras lived. Billy the Kid among them.

The party, day after tomorrow, had to have a number of dumb things like games and hamburgers and cakes and candles. Well, actually there wasn't anything wrong with candles on a cake; it was just the embarrassing singing. Mr. and Mrs. Shaw loved the singing. They'd be there beaming like Fred and Wilma Flintstone admiring their little Pebbles. The fifth-grade girls would chime in, screeching on purpose, singing the silly verses like "How old are you?/You live in a zoo./You look like a monkey./And you smell like one too."

But how to get Billy O'Hara there without inviting his stupid friends Brian and Gino? You couldn't just ask *one* boy. It would be too obvious. But Miami didn't exactly trust Brian and Gino. Or like them, for that matter. Brian had a filthy mouth, and Gino boasted of stealing money. The Shaws weren't the Rockefellers. Was there a way to tell Mrs. Shaw to lock up her valuables without raising too much suspicion?

Billy was a sweetheart. He combined all the best things in a boy, Miami thought. He was funny. Smart. And cute. Like *real* cute. Next to him, Brian looked like a reject from a funny farm. And Gino might be sexy in a pasta-commercial kind of way. But the verdict among the fifth-grade girls was unanimous: Good looks disguising a bad attitude was *bad news*. Why Billy hung around Gino and Brian was a mystery. But boys were mysteries, anyway. The *real* mystery was that *one* could be as nice as Billy.

Miami's best friend, Patty Geoghagen, had sidled up to him on the way back from First Friday Stations of the Cross a few weeks earlier. She'd said, in a suitably non-committal way, "If someone really liked you, would you want to know about it? I'm just asking as a point of interest. Supposing."

"Theoretically," mused Billy, looking off into the muddy hedges. "I'd have to think about it. You mean a lot?"

"A *lot*," said Patty. "In fact: tons."

"Oh," said Billy suddenly. "You mean Miami? She's okay, I guess."

The girls puzzled over Billy's remark later: Did it mean he'd accept an invitation to Miami's birthday party? For everyone knew she was having a party. She'd been dangling the prospects of an invitation in front of her class-mates for a month. A *big* party. It had come up in religion class, even: What were the laws about having birthday parties during Lent? Was it really right?

"You can't choose your birthday," began Miss Zebrew-ski, their teacher. "Miami can because she doesn't know when her birthday is!" the class screamed. "If April sixth has been agreed as the day to celebrate the presence of God's grace in Miami's life, that's her birthday," replied Miss Zebrewski. "It wouldn't be right not to join with her in her happiness."

"But what about eating birthday cake if you've given up dessert for Lent?" they wanted to know. Miss Zebrewski opined that a small piece, most of it left on the paper plate, would be polite. From that they deduced that a larger piece with ice cream would be more polite, and gobbling down everything and asking for seconds would be exemplary.

But then the other problem. How could Miami set about impressing Billy O'Hara if Garth was hanging around? Garth idolized big boys. He'd never let them alone. Miami couldn't quite imagine what Garth might actually inter-rupt, but she knew it would be romantic. Garth would be grinning that face he always made when an Instamatic camera got aimed at him, the face with the high-arched eyebrows and the gleeful smile. He'd swing on Billy's arms and crowd him with cake and jokes. Oh, she loved Garth and everything, but enough was enough. There was going to be *no Garth* at this party. She was putting her foot down about it.

"Miami!" It was Mrs. Shaw's voice, spiraling up to

44

the tower room, in the come-and-set-the-table tone. Mrs. Shaw had some weird idea that everyone doing chores all the time made people feel wanted and needed. I don't need to feel *that* needed, Miami thought. But with the hopes for wearing rhinestone earrings on Saturday still alive, she swung shut the window. Obedient Miami. Good Miami.

"Miami!"

"All *right*!" shrieked Miami from three floors away. Or maybe that was the do-your-homework-before-supper tone. And thinking of homework, Miami was suddenly visited by a stroke of brilliance.

She had the answer.

There was a project, a stupid geography project everyone had been assigned a month ago. It was due on Monday. Naturally she hadn't begun it yet. She could claim to forget her geography book this weekend. She could bully Patty Geoghagen into forgetting hers too. Then there was no reason why she shouldn't call Billy O'Hara on the phone! A business call, no sweat! Could I borrow your geography book? Billy was a brain, but the nice kind, not snotty. Sure, Miami, when should I drop it by? How about six on Saturday evening? The party would be in full swing. It would only be courteous to invite him in. And Gino and Brian would be off somewhere else, breaking into the church poor boxes or doing whatever bad kids did on a Saturday evening.

It was brilliant. It was flawless. All that was left to figure out was how to get rid of Garth. In her excitement she forgot to be scared of the shaky ladder and dropped into the gloom and murk of the attic with an energetic thud.

45

She barreled along the halls and pounded down the worn front stairs, almost running into Garth.

"The king's dead," said Garth excitedly.

"We don't have a king, Einstein, we have a president," she said, diving for the phone in the hall to call Patty and tell her of the plan to get Billy to the party without his hoody friends. The little girls had been set on a blanket in front of the TV. They had their thumbs in their mouths and were looking stupidly around. Garth jollied them up by doing a little dance that consisted of lifting his feet up lightly and dropping them quickly, as if stepping on coals. "The black people have a king, and he's dead," he sang.

"Will you keep it down?" said Miami in an aggrieved voice. Her finger went wheeling around the rotary dial and then froze halfway through the number. She had turned away to give her voice some privacy and looked down the hall past the bulge of coats hanging on hooks, into the kitchen. There was a smell of macaroni and cheese and Meister's excellent all-beef homemade franks boiling on the stove. In the steam, sweeping up from the open pot, stood Mrs. Shaw. The heels of her hands were pressed deep into her eye sockets. Her shoulders were shaking. A little wail, not unlike the kind Fanny and Rachelle made when they were annoyed, came out of her mouth. "Holy Mother of God," said Miami. "Will you look at that. Yikes."

She set the receiver on the cradle and leaned back to be out of sight. She'd never seen Mrs. Shaw cry. Mrs. Shaw was cheery. She believed in the power of positive thinking. A smile was her umbrella. She kept her sunny side up, up. Not only that, she blathered on about it. She was proud of being upbeat. She liked herself that way. She thought it might catch on with Miami, who was naturally a little sour, a handful of burrs in a family bouquet of wildflowers.

But Miami had been with the Shaws what, five, six years now? And Mrs. Shaw had never so much as had her eyes mist over. So what was this private display of blubbering? It was embarrassing. When Mrs. Shaw reached for a paper towel to blow her nose, Miami slipped into the living room. She cuddled the little girls, who were unused to her attentions and stopped being annoying and began to coo and bubble over her. Garth was saying, "Maybe I'll be the black king when I grow up."

"That's awfully confident, to assume you're going to grow up," said Miami. "You won't make it to six the way you're keeping on. I'll see to that. A great big rock rolled off the roof into your wading pool this summer. Good-bye, Garth."

"Oh," said Garth, used to Miami's sarcastic tone of voice, knowing she hardly meant it, "that's what you think. You just don't want me to come to your party. But I am."

"But sweetheart honey-bunny sugarlips doll, you don't want to come to my boring old party."

"Oh, yes I do," said Garth firmly. "And you can't stop me. Just because you think you're so hot."

"I am," said Miami. "Hot as hell. I love myself."

"I'm telling," said Garth. "Mommy!" he screeched. "Miami sweared!"

47

"No, don't go in there—" Miami raised herself to her knees, tumbling the toddlers off her lap. But Garth had barreled toward the kitchen. He slowed down at the sight of Mrs. Shaw. Then, stupider or braver than Miami, he catapulted himself into Mrs. Shaw's arms and gave her kisses one two three.

By the time Mr. Shaw got home from work at last, Miami had worked out what was going on. Some Negro guy had been shot and killed. Martin Luther King, Jr. "He's not a king, his *name* is King," she'd finally snapped at Garth, whose normal placid way had been stirred up by the fuss.

"But he's like a king, that's why it's on the news," said Garth. "A black king. Like me."

Mrs. Shaw finished crying and began talking. Miami preferred the crying. This was a mammoth lecture: numbers forty-seven and twenty-five and eighty-eight all rolled up in one. Martin Luther King, Jr.: A brave campaigner for the rights of American blacks. A man of God. All people are created equal. "I have a dream," said Mr. Shaw, looking soberly at Garth as if the little twerp had a clue to what was going on. "I have a dream that my four little children will one day live in a nation where they will not be judged by the color of their skins but by the content of their characters."

Garth looked at his skin color. Miami preferred hers: pale, although Garth could wear deep purples and reds that made her face look washed out.

Mrs. Shaw was wiping sauerkraut off Rachelle and Mr. Shaw was doing the same for Fanny. "We may have to postpone your party, dear," said Mrs. Shaw.

"*What?*"

You heard me."

"Why?"

"There'll be a memorial service for Dr. King."

"He's a *doctor too?*" said Garth, mouth open with joy.

"He isn't a personal member of our family!" cried Miami. "What're we gonna do, fly to wherever they just kill like that and act like crazy people? I'd be so embarrassed!"

"The cathedral will have a service, I'm sure," said Mr. Shaw, who worked for the Church in some mysterious capacity having to do with banking and budgets. "They're already lining up something for Saturday evening. Sorry, sweetheart, but your mother's right. We must go and pay our respects and pray for his soul. He's a good man, a hero, and he needs our prayers."

"If he's so good, why's he need *our* prayers?" Miami was getting loud, and the little girls began to whimper. She was going to dig her heels in over this! "It's not fair! It's my birthday party on Saturday! You promised! He isn't even a *Catholic*!"

"Honey, it can't be helped. We'll have your birthday party next weekend."

"But that's the beginning of spring break!" And the O'Haras would be going to Pennsylvania over spring break, Miami already knew. "It *can't* be then! It has to be Saturday!"

"This is an emergency, and in an emergency everybody has to pull together and make sacrifices," said Mrs. Shaw. Her tone was changing. "It will mean something to Garth that we go."

"You don't care, do you, Garth? You can come to my

49

party. Promise!" A last-minute change of tactics. "You're my favorite little brother. I'll let you have all the hot water in the bath tonight."

"You were going to smush me with a giant rock," said Garth.

"I was only *joking*," said Miami, grinning broadly, with painful brightness, as proof.

"It doesn't matter what Garth says," said Mr. Shaw. "Honey, try to be grown up about this. We're going to go as a family to the memorial service. Dr. King deserves our honoring him that way. It will be important to Garth, later on, to know he was there and we were there with him. That's what Dr. King was working for. That's what we're doing."

"We're *not*!"

"Discussion is over," said Mr. Shaw, more tired than annoyed. "That'll do, Miami Shaw."

"I hate you all," said Miami. "With a very special hate. You have just ruined the rest of my life. Thank you very much with whipped cream and a cherry on top." She pushed away from the table and ran back to the tower. No one called after her or followed with a worried look to see if she was going to pitch herself out the window. What did they care! Just to spite them she wouldn't even do it. She'd stay alive and inflict herself on them for the rest of their natural days. The big, fat, stupid jerks. Garth more than anyone.

Two evenings later Mr. and Mrs. Shaw and Miami and Garth drove downtown to the Cathedral of the Immaculate

50

Conception. Patty had come over to baby-sit Fanny and Rachelle. Miami huddled as far into her corner of the car as she could. She wore a scarf on her head even though the teachers said you didn't have to do that anymore. She didn't want anyone she knew to see her.

Garth was already over the novelty of a black king and could feel in his bones a long, boring church evening ahead. At first he had tried to jolly Miami up by dancing, but Mr. and Mrs. Shaw were so drawn and sorrowful that soon he just gave up and looked morose, too.

The church was packed; folks crowded into the aisles and the choir loft. It wasn't even a holy day of obligation or a Sunday. Miami didn't listen much to the readings or the sermon, but she stood on the kneeler to see around as far as she could. The place was full of nuns. Some had the new modern habits, but a lot of them were sticking to the old crowlike gowns and bibs. There were even a couple of dark, sensuous-looking sisters in pale blue veils with gold embroidery, whose habits were wrapped like sheets around their waists. They wore brass bangles and had red dots on their foreheads. If I were ever dumb enough to want to be a nun, that's the kind I'd be, thought Miami.

Every Catholic in Albany must be here. There were black people and white people, and yellow, and everything in between. Mrs. Jenkins, the witch from next door, was two pews over. The O'Haras, all nine of them, were there. Billy included. So that was all right; he wouldn't have been able to come over with the geography book anyway.

They all sang together. Even Miami sang. "We shall

overcome," they sang, and held hands in church. She held Garth's hand. "I still hate you," she whispered to him in a loving tone. "I hate you, too," he said, "but don't you hate this even more? It's so *boring*." They squeezed each other's hands in joyful contempt. Mr. Shaw and Mrs. Shaw were crying, the Bobbsey twins of South Allen Street. The whole thing was totally embarrassing. "Oh deep in my heart, I do believe that we shall overcome someday."

Part Three
SMITHEREENS

Underwater, Alice was no deafer than anyone else. Velvet silence. Liquid light. What she could see of the world was a broad-brimmed plate; she wore it like a hat. A hat decorated with scraggly pines, run around with ribbons of cloud, pinned with skewers of sunlight. Yet for all that, it had no weight. She jostled her hips this way and that way, as if doing a hootchy-kootchy dance, and the world wheeled overhead in perfect balance.

Then she shot up for air with a *whoosh*.

The world clicked back into place. The shallows of the lake were churned by a hundred splashing, shrieking girls. Their screams knotted together into a big ache in Alice's brain. The counselors—nuns in training, mostly, though stylish in pedal pushers and culottes—paced the dock, blowing whistles whenever anyone's life was threatened by too much watery exuberance. "Fabia Lanahan! Stop doing that to Mary Jane Jones!" Alice flicked her hair expertly back with a toss of her head and grinned wildly at no one. Then she plunged deep into her element.

It was the third day of her two weeks at Camp Saint Theresa. The weather was good, the food disgusting and plentiful, and nobody else in her cabin came from the Sacred Heart Home for Girls. Some of them were such chatterers they hadn't even realized yet that Alice couldn't speak well. So she sat on the bunk at night, making a wallet from prepunched plastic leather stitched with plastic cord for Sister Vincent de Paul, if she ever came back. The cabin leader was a large woman named Sally. She believed in regular bone-crushing hugs, morning, noon, and night, and the girls submitted as a kind of penance. Other than having to satisfy Sally's need to feel motherly, Alice found camp safe enough. Of the stink-hole bathrooms—no more than toilet seats perched above gaping holes—it was best not to think.

Alice wasn't used to being on her own as much as camp allowed. For as long as she could remember, there'd been nuns hovering within a few feet, encouraging, reprimanding, consoling. A mobile forest of women shaped more or less like Christmas trees, though done in black and white instead of jeweled colors. (The nuns at the Sacred Heart Home for Girls had not yet embraced the new stylish habits, with their scandalously shorter skirts and civilian-style blouses.) Nuns were a fact of life, like crucifixes marking their holy quadrants on the walls, or telephone lines crossing the sky in imprecise musical staffs. Nuns persisted. They weren't so much a motif in Alice's life as an element of nature, like air or dust or birds.

So down, down, into the lake the color of liquid Prell, and Alice was like the pearl in the TV commercial that dropped slowly, silently. On its own agenda, as Sister John Boss would say. Alice propelled herself like a frog, like an Egyptian doing the bent-arm dance as a swimming stroke. Alice could keep her eyes open underwater. She was as sharp as Flipper. There, for instance, through the gloom: There was Naomi Matthews pretending to swim with little pouncing hand motions hitting the water. Alice could see her feet touch down for nervous assurance every eight seconds or so. The big cheat.

She butted up into Naomi's side. Naomi gave a little squeal even Alice could hear. Alice stood up, water streaming down her hair. "Oh, Naomi. Sorry."

"Watch where you're going, clumsy," said Naomi. She was trying to swim without getting her golden mane wet.

"Swim tag! You're it!" screamed Alice, and splashed Naomi in the face with water. She tapped Naomi lightly on the shoulder and darted away with a muscular side-stroke. But Naomi wasn't biting. "Oh, Alice, *grow up*," she groaned. "I'd like to take a calm swim for a moment if I can."

"*Can* you swim?" said Alice daringly. "Don't look like any kind of swimming to me."

"Taking a break on your speech lessons for the summer, I guess," said Naomi deftly. "I can't quite make out your comment so bye-bye for now." She fake-dog-paddled away. Even her shoulders rose like little porcelain doorknobs over the water. She couldn't fool a blind person with that act, thought Alice scornfully. At least there's one thing I can do better than Naomi.

Alice had been surprised to see Naomi here, at the jamboree barbecue that opened the two-week camp session. Naomi had triumphed in the Sacred Heart–Saint Mary's joint production of *My Fair Lady*. Naomi had gone to glory in her half of the role, as Eliza Doolittle transformed into an articulate lady. Then she had moved out to live with the Harrigans. She'd taken all her things in a gray suitcase with the stitching coming out of the leather reinforcements. Alice had watched her leave. Mr. Harrigan had carried the suitcase to the car; he was so short it almost dragged on the sidewalk. Mrs. Harrigan had fluffed and plumped and kissed the air around Naomi, as if terrified yet to come in real contact, in case Naomi would change her mind before the getaway car had a chance to roar into the sunset. It seemed like a living nightmare to Alice, watching from the window on the stairs. Naomi looked more embarrassed than anything else.

She'd sent back a couple of letters to say she missed everyone. "Even Alice!" she'd added in a PS. "Can ya believe it?" She'd told of a life of great luxury. Her own bedroom. A new school. Freedom to call up friends on the telephone. Most enviable of all, her own alarm clock with a *transistor radio* in it. "Pop music is fab," she'd reported. "Ya should hear it! Ya'd love it."

"Her grammar is deteriorating," clucked Sister Francis de Sales. "You girls would do best not to envy poor Naomi too much. There's no equaling the kind of advantages you have, believe me."

On the whole, the girls did believe her. Naomi Matthews was the kind of girl things happened to, that was all. She'd probably grow up to have a cooking show on TV or something professional like that. But there could be deep sorrow in the future, ready to snare her when she got too happy. Especially if she forgot she'd started out in a girls' home like the rest of them. The girls left behind were patient. They could wait for fate or the devil to trip Naomi up. The more joy she had in youth, the worse it would be for her later. They pitied her, really.

At the opening barbecue, Alice was astounded to be lassoed with a pair of sunburned arms, to have her face burnished by an ebullient crisp structure of hair. The permanent wave was a novelty, but the color could only be Naomi Matthews. And there she was, acting like a long-lost best friend. "Alice Colossus!" she was shouting. "What're you doing here!"

"You know," said Alice, mumbling more than usual in her surprise. "The girls of Sacred Heart get to go to Camp Saint Theresa. You did, too."

"My parents thought I'd love to do something from my old life," Naomi babbled on, "and I said, well, why not Camp Saint Theresa? I hoped somebody I knew would be here! Are you around for more than one session?"

"No," said Alice.

"Me either," said Naomi. "What a gyp. It's not as if they don't have the money. They just love me so much they can't bear for me to be gone for more than two weeks."

"Oh," said Alice. "How's the lady? The lady acting like a mother, but she don't do it so good?"

"My mom," said Naomi severely. "She's fine. She's a little—uh. Well, she's not exactly Donna Reed. I mean, she cries a lot. She's okay. How's Sister Vincent de Paul? She back yet?"

"Not yet."

"Anyone else here from home? I mean from the home?"

"Ruth Peters and some of her dormitory friends are in the junior camp."

And just then Ruth Peters had run up, having sighted Naomi from across a couple of picnic tables. She burbled like a water cooler. With a shriek of joy she climbed into Naomi's lap and began to suck her thumb for all it was worth. Ruth hadn't liked Naomi much, but she was already homesick and glad to see another familiar face. After a couple of minutes she switched to Alice's lap.

"Well," said Naomi, "better go back to my table. See you around, Alice."

"No—don't go!" protested Ruth, who was capable of having a screaming fit at the slightest separation from anyone she knew.

"Only over there," said Naomi. "Honestly. She hasn't changed a bit, has she?" She winked at Alice. Alice felt faintly affronted by the wink. It had only been six months. How much was a now-five-year-old supposed to change in six months? Yet Naomi seemed to have become a certified teenager. Even her breasts seemed more confident.

Naomi had figured out who was who and latched on to a squadron of slightly older girls, who sneaked lipstick on at night though it wasn't allowed. Alice made the mistake, only once, of trying to hang around with them during a free period. They'd arched their eyebrows the first time she spoke and exchanged glances with Naomi. Alice had wandered away then, down to the lakefront, to immerse herself in a lake that didn't express any objection to her. And her spirits righted themselves there.

So for a week she stayed more or less on her own. With her long legs, she was an asset on a basketball team and enjoyed the evening game when the supper slop and after-dinner announcements were done. In the skirmishes between the eight girls on each team, a faint gray dust was raised from the bare soil on which they played. The dust hung in the sloping light, and Alice lunged through it dribbling and dodging, but not so engaged that she didn't suddenly remember the strange light in the kitchen on the morning when the retreat center burned down. Alice made a basket. Maybe the wreck of the retreat house was around here somewhere? It had been in the mountains, a couple of hours by school bus, like Camp Saint Theresa. "Way to go, Naomi!" screamed her teammates, who seemed to have confused Alice with her more glamorous acquaintance. How they did this was a mystery, as Naomi was giving Alice a wide berth now.

That was the first week. Then the camp director announced a talent show to be held on the night before the session ended. Naomi cornered Alice on the way out of the mess hall and said, "I got a great idea! You and me could do the Eliza Doolittle thing! We already know our parts. You can sing 'Wouldn't It Be Loverly' as 'Life Would Be So Heavenly' and then go offstage, and I'll come on and sing 'I Could Have Danced All Night.' But we got to find someone who knows how to play the piano or something."

"Nah," said Alice. "Once was enough."

"We'll be brilliant," said Naomi.

"It makes me feel stupid to be the dumb one."

"First prize," said Naomi, "is fifty bucks. We could split it."

"Well," said Alice. "We got to give some to the piano guy."

"Deal," said Naomi.

"Deal," said Alice with a sinking feeling.

In the second week of the session Alice tried to become chatty with Sally the cabin leader. As a nun in training she might know something about Sister Vincent de Paul. But as far as Alice could figure, if Sally was aiming at being a nun she wasn't going to make it. She smoked cigarettes and sang Beatles songs to herself while she pinned her hair around plastic rollers the size of beer cans. She said to Alice, "In this business I know as few nuns as I can get away with." At least that's what Alice thought she said. "Sister Vincent de Paul?" said Alice again faintly. "Never had the pleasure. What order is she?" asked Sally. "Redemption." "Hah!" said Sally contemptuously, "Redemptions! The living end!"

Naomi had identified a piano player, a timid girl from Schaghticoke called Wendy Beasley. Naomi had threatened to pull off Wendy's bathing suit in the lake if she didn't agree to accompany them in selections from *My Fair Lady*. Wendy, suffering a nearly terminal case of modesty, succumbed to the pressure. Alice thought that family life wasn't having a healthy influence on Naomi Matthews. "By the way," she said one evening, "are you Naomi Harrigan now?"

"Ow oo Naomi Howwigan," parroted Naomi. "Sorry, Alice, couldn't resist. Really, you make a perfect Eliza Doolittle. I wonder if you will ever meet a real Henry Higgins to teach you how to talk?" She didn't answer the question, and Alice didn't have the nerve to ask it again.

Costumes! Sally found an old black-lace mantilla some lady had left behind in the rustic Chapel in the Pines, which was no more than a concrete floor with a roof and some banners made out of felt, saying PRAISE and REJOICE and BE GLAD. The black lace thing made a perfect shawl. Now all Alice needed was a basket of flowers and a crummy skirt. The kitchen help came up with a wicker picnic basket, and there were more black-eyed Susans and Queen Anne's lace and daisies in the fields than a whole battalion of Eliza Doolittles could use. Sally also sacrificed a perfectly good gray skirt for Alice's costume, which was nice of her, Alice had to admit, but the sacrifice locked Alice into having to go through with the performance. Sally cut holes in the skirt with a Swiss army knife and smeared ashes from the campfire all over it. "You look like a perfect wreck!" she exclaimed when Alice did herself up in shawl, skirt, and basket.

It was a bit harder finding ball gown material for Eliza, as played by Naomi. Wendy Beasley suggested a nun's habit, but that was out of the question. In the end they rigged up something with a sheet from the infirmary and a gold belt that was really Sally's necklace. Alice thought

Naomi looked like the bride of Frankenstein with all that hair, but then Sally fussed over it with pins and hair spray, and it all stood on top of her head like a flock of birds densely packed together with glue, soft and hard at the same time.

"You know I hate this," said Alice as they stood in the pantry, waiting for their turn.

"Twenty bucks," said Naomi inspiringly. "Think what you can do with your share of the first prize. Twenty bucks."

"And now Alice Colossus to perform *My Fair Lady*, as the Cockney flower girl Eliza Doolittle!" screeched Sally through the ancient PA system.

Wendy Beasley lurched over the keyboard as if she were having stomach cramps and battered the opening chords loud enough for Alice to catch the musical cue. She sang while squatting like an Iroquois and pretending to rub her hands before a fire. Actually my voice is pretty good, she thought. Nobody was laughing, which was an improvement over the time she'd done it with the boys from Saint Mary's of Albany. "And life could be so heavenly!"

Ruth Peters came up to the edge of the stage. "Alice!" she cooed. "Hi, Alice!" Everyone laughed.

Alice just went on with the next line. Ruth remembered the words, too, and sang along as she scrambled up the steps. She held Alice's hand, and they sang to the end of the song. The little dance Alice had planned was ruined, but it was okay. Ruth was having such a good time.

When she finished, the girls began to shout and cheer. They were a very enthusiastic audience. They hammered their feet on the floor and called in rhythm, "NA-O-MI!

62

NA-O-MI!" Alice would have preferred their calling "AL-ICE, AL-ICE," but as long as her part was done she didn't care. She swept off stage and Sally intoned, "Eliza Doolittle makes friends with a speech therapist named Henry Higgins, who teaches her how to speak clearly and then takes her to a fancy ball. Naomi Matthews as Eliza coming home from the ball."

So her last name *was* still Matthews. Hmmm. Alice wondered why. She watched Naomi twirl in from the dark shadows in her silly-looking bedsheet. The audience oohed and aahed. Wendy Beasley slaved away at the crisp runs of the introduction, and Naomi began to shrill out her part. When she got to the final line, she improvised a cancan kick by picking up her sheets and jackknifing her legs out like a single demented Rockette. The crowd shrieked—praising, rejoicing, and being glad. Naomi warbled out her last note, squeezing every second she could out of it, and even Alice in the mercy of her deafness could tell Naomi was a half-tone sharp. The girls of the 1968 second summer session of Camp Saint Theresa weren't, on the whole, as discriminating as Alice. They went wild.

They stamped. They wolf-whistled. They called, "NA-O-MI! NA-O-MI!" Naomi beckoned Alice back on stage for another bow. Alice and Ruth Peters came out. Ruth bowed more times than anyone.

Third prize went to Cabin Saint Dymphna, for singing "Puff the Magic Dragon" in harmony. Third prize had no money attached. Naomi and Alice got second prize, which was worth only twenty-five bucks—ten bucks each and five for Wendy Beasley. Then Wendy Beasley walked off with the first prize of fifty dollars. Without so much as a

63

word of friendly warning, she had entered herself as a separate act. She had played "Malaguea," all eight pages of it, in just under ninety seconds, even the slow part. The traitor.

But Alice hadn't ever expected to have as much as twenty bucks, so it wasn't too big a disappointment to pocket ten. Naomi was so thrilled with cleaning up what she called the popular support of Camp Saint Theresa that she didn't even mind Alice trailing along afterward when she met her glitzier friends. "You know you have a good voice," said Naomi, not too grudgingly. "I mean you can't understand much, but it has a pretty sound."

"You've got a *great* voice, Naomi," said one of the other girls in an enthusiastic tizzy, bouncing and beaming fatuously at Alice.

"I'm not Naomi," said Alice.

"She didn't say Naomi," said Naomi. "She said Naomi."

From time to time, Alice found herself in a hearing dead end. Usually she just shrugged and accepted the fact that she couldn't figure out what was going on. But Ruth Peters was still clutching Alice's left hand. With her higher voice she clarified for Alice what was being said. "She's calling you Miami, Alice," said Ruth. "Not Naomi."

"Miami?" said Alice.

"That's what they were all shouting when you finished," said Naomi. "I didn't get it, either. What's Miami got to do with the price of beans?"

"Isn't that her name?" said Pam, one of the glitzier girls.

"It's *Alice*," said Naomi. "Everybody knows that."

"No," said Pam. "Why'd you tell everybody it was Miami?"

"I never did," said Alice.

"You did too."

"Nobody don't talk to me," said Alice. "So, like, when?"

"When you won the basketball competition, most dunks from a standing start," said the girl in an aggrieved voice. "Stop pulling our legs, Miami. Just because you can sing."

"*What* basketball thing?"

"Last session, the basketball thing."

"I wasn't here last session," said Alice.

"She wasn't here last session," said Naomi. "You've got a screw loose, Pam."

"You were too," said Pam. A couple of the other girls nodded and shrugged in a single motion. "Don't give me that."

"I was not," said Alice. "I was home."

There were marshmallows over an open fire. Most of the camp had flocked there after the talent show. Alice, Naomi, Ruth, and the older girls stood aside, mired in their misunderstandings. Tiny red sparks went zigging up, burning out before they got even eight or ten feet high. Above, the stars were salty white, and the wind rushed through the trees with the sound of water. "All I know," said the challenged Pam, who could be as energetically offended as she could be delighted, "is that I was here for both sessions, and Miami won the basketball jump award.

And there were enough girls there then who can back me up on this now. That's why people were chanting Mi-am-i! when you were finished singing."

"I thought they were saying *Na-o-mi*," said Alice.

"They said that later," said Pam. The other girls were drifting toward the fire.

"How'd she speak?" said Naomi suddenly.

"Regular," said Pam. "Why?"

"Alice can't speak regular," said Naomi. "She's got a defect. Her tongue is too big or something, and she's deaf."

"Only partly," said Alice sharply.

"You mean that's not an act?" said Pam. "I thought she was just being silly."

"Ha-ha," said Alice coldly, and turned toward the fire.

"Sorry," called Pam. "I didn't mean it like that."

The fire wasn't any fun. It brought back too many memories of the retreat house burning down and Sister Vincent de Paul getting scorched. Alice wandered out onto the dock. The lake was a dark mirror. Above it, the stars were tiny as grains of sand, yet they seemed to light up the whole sky. The lake surface, though bright in its own way, was too active to reflect the stars. It stirred in its bed, almost imperceptibly. Alice had an idea of diving into the water, even with her stupid Eliza Doolittle costume on. They hadn't even been clapping for her, but for some girl named Miami they were mixing her up with. Every little happiness got shattered into smithereens. Nothing was fair. She hoped she never saw Naomi Matthews again. She couldn't wait till tomorrow to go home.

THE TWILIGHT ZONE

Alice did not consider herself a quick thinker. But a few days later, back in the baking summer heat of the third floor of the Sacred Heart Home for Girls, she had to congratulate herself on her initiative. She was looking at the addresses she'd collected at camp. On a scrap of notebook paper were scrawled the home addresses of Sally the reluctant novice, an RFD route in Feura Bush; of Wendy Beasley in Schaghticoke; of Naomi Matthews in Watervliet. At the bottom, printed in Sally's neatest nun-in-training script, was the address of Miami Shaw: 86 South Allen Street. Albany.

It had been easy to find the Miami Shaw address. Alice had simply told Sally the truth. People were confusing Alice with a camper who'd been enrolled in the previous session. Alice wanted to write her a letter. Could Sally dig up the address in the office? The extra hug Alice gave Sally ahead of time was only mildly a bribe. When Sally came back with the goods, the next hug was genuine.

Alice sat on her bed. During the summer the home was unusually quiet; some girls were always away at the camp, and the sisters rotated supervising the rest. Alice chewed on the long pointed collar of her striped shirt. She told herself: Think. Think. But she wasn't really sure what she should be thinking about.

Why and how there could be somebody living ten miles away who looked like her, that was what to think about. But Alice couldn't get past just the fact of it. Was it really true? How could it be? It seemed like a miracle. It would've been good to be able to drift downstairs to the kitchen now and peel potatoes with Sister Vincent de Paul. The subject could've come up. What would Sister Vincent de Paul have to say about it? Try as she might, Alice couldn't imagine. In her mind Sister Vincent de Paul opened her mouth with an expression of mighty strong opinion, but there wasn't any way of telling what the opinion was. Short of asking her, of course. But how to do that?

It was six months. Six long months since Sister Vincent de Paul had left. Now the sun pelted upstate New York with blasts of hot air, lashings of buttery heat. The ice-rain storm was a distant impossibility, an adventure story that had already become boring by overtelling. Now the tar on the roof of the home grew sticky and melted in the heat, and the smell eddied in through the gray screens at nighttime, followed by the sweet vegetable-rot aroma of the weedy saplings that grew in the alley. It was a different season, and Alice supposed she was a different person. But she would've liked Sister Vincent de Paul there anyway. A new nun, a young, smooth-faced, cranky one named Sister Paul the Hermit, had come in and taken over the cooking. The girls called her Sister Paul the Hermit Crab. That her name was somewhat like Sister Vincent de Paul's made Alice anxious, as if one nun could blot out another just like that, by having a similar name.

So Alice sat and pondered. In the absence of Sister Vincent de Paul she had few choices. She kept the folded-up address list and the ten-dollar bill she'd won as her share of second prize in the talent show in the little Camp Saint Theresa wallet, which she'd decorated with a holy card. The bill and the holy card and the address list seemed to operate on each other like ingredients in a stew. Having no other ideas, Alice decided to act.

On Thursday there was an outing to Thacher Park. Sister John Boss herself was going to drive one of the station wagons, and Sister Francis Xavier the other. Most of the girls loved to swim in the pool, especially as it was the custom to stop at the Tollhouse for ice cream on the way home. Alice signed herself up to go, and then went into the kitchen to speak with Sister Paul the Hermit.

"If I decide not to go, if I want to stay here and help you make supper, can I?" said Alice. "Sister Vincent de Paul always used to say yes."

"Oh, the trials," said Sister Paul the Hermit. "I know you're the special case, but you're going to have to speak more clearly, child of God, if you expect me to understand. They tell me you can; you're just lazy."

"I'm not lazy," shouted Alice.

"I heard *that*," said Sister Paul the Hermit. "Now what's the rest?"

Alice repeated her proposal. She was counting on Sister Paul the Hermit's being too new to have learned the system completely, and she was right. (So why'd they write on her report card that *Alice* was a slow learner when the stupid nun couldn't even figure out how things went?) "It's okay by me," said Sister Paul the Hermit. "But I'm warning you. I'm not the world's best company today. It's that time of month."

"If you don't see me here in fifteen minutes, I went swimming and don't worry," said Alice. "But you gotta sign this paper that says it's okay. Thanks, Sister Paul the Hermit."

"I wish," sighed the nun. "The hermit part, I mean."

With the permission form in hand, Alice went and dawdled in the parking lot with the other girls. Esther Thessaly and Rachel Luke were playing jump rope. "Fancy lady dressed in red, sleeps each night in a different bed. People want to know why is it, how many bedrooms did she visit. One. Two. Three." The fancy lady visited fourteen bedrooms before Esther tripped on the rope. Then the nuns swept down the concrete steps and clucked and pummeled the kids into the cars, including Alice. She waited, and just before the door closed she hopped out again. "I'm going to stay. Sister Paul the Hermit signed for me," she said. She thrust the paper at Sister John Boss, who was annoyed.

"Don't be fickle," said Sister John Boss. "Get in the car."

"I feel carsick," said Alice, and then, daringly, "It's my time of the month."

"Oh, lordy," said Sister John Boss. "I hope not. Not already. You're only a babe."

"Wanna stay home too!" screamed Ruth Peters, trying to scramble over laps to follow Alice.

"You stay where you are, Ruth. You need some sunlight," snapped Sister John Boss. "Well, all right, Alice, if you're not feeling well, go and lie down. Sister Paul the Hermit will get you an aspirin if you need one, and we'll be back in a couple of hours. I'll come up to check things over then. You understand?"

"Gotcha," said Alice.

The cars left. The neighborhood sighed in relief; it liked it when the girls went away for a while. Alice ran and found her wallet, which she had hidden under the lilac bushes. Then, remembering her expedition to Saint Mary's in February to deliver the *My Fair Lady* music, she hurried along the sidewalk to where she'd caught the bus.

Only this time she had ten bucks in her pocket. She could plan a more efficient disobedience now. She corraled all her available courage, and invented some she didn't really have, then leaned down at the window of a waiting taxicab. "I need to go to Albany, number eighty-six South Allen Street," she said. "It's an emergency."

The cab driver opened the door and said, "Jump in, sister." He didn't seem to have any problem understanding her. For a minute she wondered if he thought she was a nun. No, he was just being friendly, calling her *sister*.

"You got the cash for a ride all the way to Albany?" said the man.

"Is ten dollars enough?" said Alice.

"You'll get change," he said, and pulled the sleek yellow car out into the stream of traffic.

The window was down, and air splashed Alice's long hair into a frenzy worthy of Hollywood. The noise made talking difficult, for which she was grateful. She didn't have a plan for when she got to South Allen Street. She might just turn around and come right back. She just wanted to see where this Miami Shaw lived. It would be like knowing another possible life she could have had if she'd wanted. Who knew what it would be like? She was just curious.

There was the Hudson River, flat and brown in the heat. Kids were fishing, their lines going down into the water amid rejected car tires and a scum of greenish froth. Then came the big, white cliff-face of Montgomery Wards' warehouse, and before long the taxicab was zipping through downtown Albany traffic. Alice didn't feel as if she were pushing the limits of her guardian angel's jurisdiction this time. Albany seemed perkily familiar. There was the monumental State Capitol building. There the State Education Building with a well-behaved grove of Greek columns lined up in front. Men were walking around in short-sleeved shirts, ties loosened, buying hot dogs and Cokes at pushcarts. It made Alice feel safe, to see government guys at lunch.

Then the taxicab careered through a park, with curving roads and gentle hills, until it came out on a broad street lined with dying elm trees and huge red or yellow brick houses. "Is this South Allen Street?" asked Alice.

"No. I'm going to have to stop and ask at a gas station. It's around here somewhere," said the driver. "My regular stomping ground is Troy, dolly. Give me a sec; I'll figure it out."

The young guy at the pump answered the driver's question. For a second Alice thought it was the boy with the guitar, the one who had befriended her on the bus from Troy last winter. But before she could take a second look to be sure, the taxicab was zipping off again. Nobody in a taxicab does anything slowly, do they, thought Alice. I haven't had time for the next step to occur to me yet— and here we are. South Allen Street.

She gave the number again. The driver pulled over. "Here you are," he said, and gave her more than five dollars in change. Well! She could even afford to take a cab home! This wasn't such a difficult life out here.

She stood on the sidewalk. The house was the highest one in sight; it crowned a steep hill, the front slope of which was dense with brush and an ample supply of litter caught at its roots. A long flight of steps, made of wood and grounded in crumbling concrete, leaned to the right as it climbed the incline. Above, Alice could see the roof of a porch—the hill was too steep to see into the front yard without mounting the steps—and the house rose overhead, clapboards a little loose, windows open for the breeze, and a spike-roofed turret lifting skyward. It was the sloppiest house in the neighborhood. Alice fell in love with it.

But what was she supposed to do now, just stand there and look at it?

Before she could decide, an inflatable beach ball came bounding off the front lawn and began to roll down the steps as if trying to escape the kids who were playing with it. Alice ran forward and caught it neatly as it bounced off the lower steps, heading for sure suicide in the busy street. "Thanks," said a boy's voice overhead. Alice looked up. "I thought you were eating lunch at Patty's today," he said. He was about the size of Ruth Peters, but a different color and about a hundred years ahead in confidence. "Throw me the ball."

"Hi," said Alice.

"Hi," he said. "What'd Patty do to your hair now? You look like Mrs. Munster."

"Who're you?" she said.

"Come on, Miami. Give me the ball," he answered.

She walked up the steps slowly. She'd never felt more in a dream than now, not even when she swam underwater. The whole world seemed to be underwater, or shot through with a new kind of air, or vibrating to an earthquake. "Patty who?"

"Why're you talking like that, you practicing for Halloween already?" said the boy. "Guess what. Mommy said we can go to the drive-in tonight and see *The Singing Nun*."

"Great," said Alice. "Just perfect."

The boy looked at her. "You got different clothes," he said.

"I got a different name," she told him.

"What is it?"

"Alice. What's yours?"

74

He looked worried. "It's *Garth*," he told her. "Why you doing this?"

"I'm not doing it," she said.

"I mean talking funny and looking funny?"

"I can't help it."

"What happened to you?"

"I don't know," she said. "What happened to you?"

"Nothing, I just was playing with the ball." He reached out and touched Alice's hair. "How'd you get your hair like that?"

"It's a miracle," she said, because he was starting to look terrified.

"Cut it *out*, Miami," he said. "I don't like this game."

"I'm sorry, Garth. It's not a game."

"Don't say *Gowth*."

"I can't help it." But she didn't mean to scare him. "Is Miami your sister?"

"Of course you're my sister!" Now he was getting mad. "This is dumb. I'm going in."

"No, don't! Please. Stay here with me."

"I don't like you like this," he said, his lower lip sticking out. "Stop it."

"I can't."

"Are you bewitched?" he asked, eyes widening.

"I don't know," she said. "It feels something like that."

"Will you get better if I kiss you?"

"It don't work like that this time." Boy, he was quicker than she was. Alice was exhausted with trying to answer him honestly. Her mind could hardly keep up, much less race ahead and figure out what should happen next. But things seemed to have been taken out of her control now that she was here. She felt as if she might go drifting skyward like a saint in the paintings.

It had often occurred to her that maybe saints didn't have as much choice in being saints as all that. How could you stop yourself if you started drifting to heaven in a religious trance? Grab hold of a tree? Think evil thoughts so you would plummet earthward? If you were a saint, you probably didn't know how to think evil thoughts.

"Who the—?"

Alice spun around. There was the girl, standing on the top step, carrying a couple of record albums under her arm. She looked like Alice in the mirror only with shorter hair, and her ears were pierced. "Garth, what's going on?" shouted the girl. One of the records slipped out of its sleeve and went rolling down the steps the way the beach ball had.

"I'm going to get Mommy," said Garth, and shot into the house, the screen door slamming behind him.

"I don't believe it," said the girl.

"I don't believe it," said Alice. "You're Miami."

"Who're you? What're you doing here?" She wouldn't stop shouting.

"Don't be so mean," said Alice. "I just came to look at you."

"What've you been doing, sucking on ice cubes?"

"My tongue is too fat for my mouth!" Alice shouted back. "Shut up about it, will you!"

The girl flinched; her body seemed to jerk from knees to dangling earrings. Alice could tell at once this was a big mistake. She should have written a letter or made a phone call. The girl was having a nervous breakdown. Miami

76

Shaw was having a nervous breakdown. "I'll go home now," said Alice. "I'm sorry."

"Don't you move. I'm calling the cops!" shouted Miami. "Mommy! *Mommy*!"

"I've got the babies in the sink, can it wait?" came a woman's voice from far inside the shadowy house. A mother's voice.

"There's a thief pretending to be me! It's a spy! It's a secret agent!" shouted Miami. "Call the cops!" She ran into the house and slammed the front door behind her so hard that the glass shattered.

"I said I'm sorry!" Alice shouted up toward the damaged door. "I'm going now! I won't come back!"

"And stay out!" The girl was crying. Really she was being a baby, Alice thought. She turned and walked down the steps to the sidewalk. At the foot of the rickety steps lay the record. It hadn't broken, miraculously. It was Simon and Garfunkel. Alice carried it back up to lay it on the porch. Maybe Miami would find it and realize it was a peace offering.

"Hold it right there," said a voice through the screen. Alice froze. "I'm coming out the side door and you, don't you move a muscle," said the voice again. "If you know what's good for you." So Alice stood still, and in a minute there appeared in the yard a woman in an apron, with two naked baby girls, one under each arm. Garth followed, hugging his beach ball, and Miami came last, scowling and sniffling and rubbing her eyes.

"I don't believe it," said the woman. "Who sent you here? Who are you?"

"Hello," said Alice. "How do you do?"

"Answer me!"

"My name is Alice Colossus. Nobody sent me here."

"Somebody must've. You'd better come inside. I don't believe this. Miami, blow your nose. Nobody on the front porch until I clean up the glass. Is that understood? Round this way, Alice. Is it Alice?"

"Alice."

She was surrounded and ushered into a hall, and up a couple of steps to a kitchen that hadn't yet been cleared of breakfast dishes. Boy, the sisters wouldn't think much of this lady's housekeeping, thought Alice. She sat on a step stool. Miami and Garth sat on an upholstered bench, and the little girls seemed to be trying to scratch each other's eyes out. The woman put the babies in separate playpens in a glassed-in porch off the kitchen and came back.

"This is very serious," she said. "You had better start at the beginning, young lady, and tell me everything."

Alice wasn't sure where the beginning was. But she told the story. The woman kept interrupting to ask nosy questions. Garth sat very still, taking the beach ball plug out with his teeth and putting it back in again with his tongue and lips. Miami stopped crying but sat with her head in her hands. When Alice finished, Miami said to her mother, "Just one question. Does this mean we don't get to go to *The Singing Nun* tonight like you *promised*?"

"Miami," said the woman, "don't push me."

The phone rang before that interesting conversation could go any further. Garth twisted away from the table and grabbed the receiver. "Hi, Daddy," he said.

"Good. . . . Good. . . . Yeah. . . . Nothing. Oh, guess what. There's another Miami, and she's here. I *think* she's staying for lunch."

Holding the receiver by its cord, he said, "Mommy, it's Daddy and he wants to talk to you now."

"I'll bet he does," said the woman dryly. Alice and Miami both leaned forward to hear what she'd say. "It's the Twilight Zone around here," she announced. "Garth was right: There's a second Miami sitting in the kitchen with the first."

Miami and Alice looked at each other. "My hair is neater than yours, and I don't sound like a broken robot," said Miami.

"Mine is longer than yours, and I'm part deaf," said Alice.

"No," said Mrs. Shaw. "It's not that. Thank God and all the saints. It's a girl. You'd better come here. She looks like a twin. She just showed up, and she scared the bejazus out of everyone. Her name is Alice, or so she says. Honey, come as quickly as you can."

"I never saw *The Singing Nun*," said Alice.

"I can play the song on the piano," said Miami.

"The babies are crying," said Alice. "Shouldn't you go pick them up?"

"Oh, let them cry, they'll only start again as soon as you put them down," said Miami. "They have one-track minds. You know your speech isn't so bad once you get used to it."

But Alice had gone out onto the porch. The little girls were still damp from being lifted out of their bath. Alice

79

found a towel in a basket of laundry and rubbed them dry, while Miami sat on the beach ball as fast and hard as she could to get all the air out of it and hide it from Garth.

In the end, Mr. Shaw came home from work early, and Sister John Bosco showed up with Father Laverty in tow. Nobody was in a very happy mood. Miami and Alice sat on the sofa. It had an Indian-print cloth thrown over it to hide where it was ripped (Alice had looked underneath to see). On the wall was a poster with a couple of priest's hands breaking a loaf of bread and the words in curlicued letters saying, "Where two or three are gathered in My name, there am I." Father Laverty even knew Mr. Shaw from before. He called him Joe, and Mr. Shaw called Father Laverty Father Kevin.

"How could you do this to us," said Sister John Boss in a voice that didn't seem to expect Alice would have the nerve to answer, and she didn't. "Do you know they had to page me at Thacher Park? Sister Paul the Hermit was beside herself with worry."

"You've kept us hopping, haven't you, Alice," said Father Laverty. "I thought your little escapade this winter would get it out of your system."

"I have a twin," said Alice. "Lookit."

"So I see," said Father Laverty. "Hello there, twin."

"Do *I* have a twin?" asked Garth. "When's he get here?"

They talked a lot. Father Laverty seemed to know as much about the Sacred Heart Home for Girls as Sister John Boss did, or maybe she was just keeping her mouth shut because she was so angry. Her lips were little purple pads like two well-chewed pieces of grape gum pressed together. Alice wasn't scared of her, just sorry that she had done a stupid thing by not going to Sister John Bosco first and telling her what had happened at camp.

So they were related. There wasn't much doubt. They were both twelve, though they'd been given different birthdays by accident. They had the same color hair, the same color eyes; they were the same height, though Alice was skinnier. They'd both started out life at the Brady Hospital and had spent their early years at Saint Catherine's Infant Home. Then Alice had had a lung ailment and had gone for treatment somewhere, and Miami had been taken by a family living in the town of Catskill. The family had gotten poor and had a divorce or something, and Miami was adopted by the Shaws when she was six.

Way back in the olden days, before they could remember, they'd been babies together, lying in next-door cribs, maybe looking at each other the way Fanny and Rachelle looked at each other. It seemed strange to Alice that she couldn't remember this, because what else so important had ever happened to her in her life?

Sister John Bosco kept shaking her head. "Alice, when you act impetuously you don't know the harm you cause." She spoke crisply. "Father Laverty, I don't think we should discuss this anymore in front of the children. It's time to let things settle in a bit. Alice, will you apologize to the Shaws and use the bathroom if you need to."

"No!" said Alice.

"Alice," said Sister John Bosco, "don't make this harder on yourself than it need be."

She hadn't realized that she didn't want to leave. The Shaws looked nice. They were a nice family! Miami was a little mean, but no worse than Naomi Matthews. Garth was cute. The little girls were adorable. Mrs. Shaw looked like a TV mother, though a bit weary around the edges and her dress could use a pressing. Mr. Shaw was handsome and kind. They had a crucifix on the wall of the dining room! What more did Sister John Boss want?

"Sister John Bosco is right, Alice," said Mr. Shaw. "It's been an exhilarating day. There can't be too many things more surprising than this. But we all need to do some thinking. You'd better get ready to go home."

"She can stay here," said Garth. "She's nicer than Miami. Let Miami go with you."

"Shut up, you little monster," said Miami hotly.

"Miami!" said the four adults.

"Mi-*a*-mi!" said Garth, mimicking them.

"This is my home, not hers!" said Miami. "And I don't want to get cheated out of that movie like I was cheated out of my birthday party!"

"Say thank you to Mrs. Shaw for being so calm," said Father Laverty. "It's a wonder nobody had a heart attack today."

"There's still time," said Sister John Bosco darkly. "Come along, Alice."

Alice stood. For an instant she thought she was going blind as well as partly deaf and dull of tongue. Then, as her eyes began to smart, she realized it was only ordinary tears starting. She let herself be led to the side door and down the rickety steps to the street, with Father Laverty on one side patting her shoulder clumsily, and Sister John Bosco holding her hand as if she were a little child. A woman next door with a garden hose said, "My word, what's the matter, Miami? Where are they taking you? Hey you, Father, Sister, where you going with our Miami?" But the three of them got in the car without answering and drove away.

Part Four

LIFE WOULD BE
SO HEAVENLY

To Miami's surprise, the trip to the drive-in wasn't canceled. After a long afternoon, which her parents spent in the kitchen with the door closed, the family went to Carroll's for hamburgers and to Carvel for soft ice cream, and then headed out on Route 20 to the drive-in. The kids all had to dress in their pajamas before leaving the house, which made it seem like Halloween in the middle of the summer. "Gee, it's too bad that girl couldn't stay and come to the movies with us," said Garth. "I mean, she knows all about nuns."

"*Garth*," said everybody.

"Well, what?" he said.

"Grow up," said Miami.

"That'll do," said Mrs. Shaw.

"Put a lid on it, Garth, it's been a long day," said Mr. Shaw.

"Sheez," he said. "I only said—"

"Garth said *sheez*," said Miami. *Sheez* was uncomfortably close to *Jesus*, which would be taking the Lord's name in vain.

"I said *cheese*," said Garth, and started to cry.

"Now let's just enjoy ourselves, shall we," said Mr. Shaw in a testy way. "Garth. Nobody's yelling at you."

"Certainly not *me*," said Miami. "I'm only reporting basic truth."

"Do I have to pull the car over and deliver a few spankings back there?" asked Mrs. Shaw, who was driving.

The sheer unlikeliness of a remark like that shut Garth and Miami up. Mrs. Shaw was the spirit of Catholic niceness most of the time.

In the next couple of days, though, the atmosphere at home was strained, to say the least. It seemed off-limits even to mention that somebody looking mighty like Miami had showed up out of nowhere. Miami spent a lot of time in her tower room, which was almost unbearably hot. She had to keep very still, except for smushing flies with a newspaper. Otherwise she was so warm she could hardly breathe.

She sat and looked out the window. She hadn't told her friend Patty Geoghagen about Alice Colossus, because Patty had just left for a vacation to visit her aunt in Ithaca. She *had* started to tell Billy O'Hara when she ran into him at the Price Chopper, but it seemed too farfetched a story to be believed among the frozen peas and pizzas. If her parents weren't ever going to bring it up again, what was the point?

"Hey, Miami," said Garth.

She jumped. "What're you doing in the attic? You're not allowed," she hissed.

"Can I come up?"

"*No.*"

"Well, come down then."

"What for?"

"I want to talk to you."

She came down the ladder. "If I ever catch you up there, so help me, you'll be minced meat, buddy."

"Yeah, yeah, yeah," he said. "Miami, I got an idea."

"What?"

"Let's ask Mommy and Daddy to adopt that other girl."

"You mean Alice," she said. "My sister."

"Well, if she's your sister, she's my sister," said Garth.

Miami didn't argue that one. He was probably right. He went on. "Don't you think that's a good idea? She could sleep in your bedroom."

"I don't know," said Miami.

"Why not? It's simple. Let's go ask them."

Miami wasn't sure she wanted Alice around. It was too creepy. The other family she'd been in for a while, the Dillons, had been given to lopsided emotions, veering from weepy embraces to loud fights and beatings. Miami thought the Shaws were a lot more comfortable. Who knew if another girl wouldn't change the pattern of things?

But suppose she'd been Alice, and Alice had been she? Wouldn't she want the girl who *had* the family to fight for getting her into it? Not even knowing Alice yet, Miami felt a dull requirement to be good to her. "Okay," she told Garth. "I guess we can try."

She waited until evening. Following fried-egg sand-

87

wiches came homemade Popsicles made of frozen Kool-Aid; it seemed a good time. "By the way," she said, making a show of sharing her Popsicle with disgusting Fanny, who was intent on slobbering all over it, "why don't we adopt that girl Alice?"

"Good idea," said Garth loudly. "Let's vote."

"Not so fast," said Mrs. Shaw.

"All in favor, say aye," said Miami. She raised Fanny's pudgy fist and squealed an *aye* as if from her. Garth followed suit with Rachelle. At least Mr. and Mrs. Shaw smiled at this, which was a start.

They continued the conversation as they did some evening yard work.

"So whaddya think about my idea?" said Miami.

"My idea," said Garth.

"Look, kids," said Mr. Shaw. "This is hard to say. But there are so many more things to think about than you realize. How much it costs to run a family of four kids already. You know how much we love you. That's why we adopted all of you. But there are laws about adoption. And it seems to be the right time to tell you that it looks like you might have a new brother or sister in a few months anyway. Well, after Christmas."

"Alice?" said Garth.

"No. A new baby."

"You don't mean Mommy's pregnant?" said Miami. "Aren't you too old? That's gross!"

Mrs. Shaw said, "I'm not too old according to my doctors. Nor my body, apparently. We were going to wait another month to tell you, to make sure we pass the first set of hurdles. But it seems you should know earlier. Sweethearts, it's going to be a real stretch to handle a family of five kids. We didn't think I could get pregnant. That's why we took all of you on. We wanted a family."

"So does one of us have to go back?" said Miami. "Why not Garth?"

"No sir, not me," said Garth. "I ain't moving."

"Well, Garth is the only really different one," said Miami. "We could trade him for Alice. Then we'd all match at least."

"Miami," said Mrs. Shaw. "If you're going to get on our nerves, you can go inside. You know what we think of talk like that. We're not going to give up any of you. However could we? We don't want to. We're a family. But we're a big family—we're going to be five kids."

"So what's one more? Alice is skinny. She won't eat a lot. She can have half of mine," said Miami. "She's my sister."

"She *is* your sister," said Mr. Shaw. "And that means she has a special place in our family, like a very extra-special cousin. But it doesn't mean she can live here. For one thing, darlings, the people who make those decisions probably just wouldn't allow it. You have to earn a certain amount per child, and while we qualified for each of you, having a new baby in the family is going to put us out of the running for any other adoptions, I'm afraid."

"How much does it cost?" said Miami. "I have forty bucks in the bank from my birthday."

"More than that." Mrs. Shaw raked up clipped grass. "Besides, Alice is going to need some pretty fancy speech therapy, maybe an operation on her tongue when she's a little older. It's a burden we can't accept; we couldn't honor it. But we'll clearly have to get to know her. She can come visit sometimes, maybe, if we all agree it's a good idea."

"You know," said Miami, "you people are real hypocrites."

"Hypocrites. What a word!" said Mr. Shaw. "Your vocabulary is improving, Miami."

"I mean it," said Miami. "What's the difference between me and Alice? I thought we were Catholics and had to love everybody. How can you make sandwiches on my plate and not make some for her too?"

"We didn't do it on purpose," said Mrs. Shaw. "I don't expect you to understand, sweetie. I expect you to be furious with us. But it just can't be helped. And Alice might not want to come into a family where there are three babies and a girl who looks just like her but doesn't have her ailments. It might make her feel inferior."

"I could help her learn to talk better, I know I could!" cried Miami. "You're just mean!"

"Me too," said Garth bravely. "But I ain't going to anybody else's family for *anything.*"

Miami ran inside and banged the screen door behind her. Garth ran after her, but she turned in the hall and shouted, "Get lost and stop following me, you creep!" So he changed his mind.

She stormed upstairs. But not all the way to the tower. She went into the bathroom on the second floor and stood by the window with the light turned out, so they wouldn't know she was there. The Shaws kept clipping their hedge and trimming their lawn as if there were no terrible crisis at hand. She hated them. It wasn't fair.

In her parents' bedroom she flopped on the chenille bedspread, and absentmindedly pulled out some of the tufts and dropped little clumps of blue cotton on the floor. What an awful week this was! She wished Patty would come back; she wished things would get back to normal. She wished lightning would come down and strike all five members of her family at once. Then she could go find Alice and they could live by themselves in Washington Park or someplace.

Are you thinking about me, Alice? she wondered. You don't even know me. But there you were all along, growing up someplace not so far away. How come I got to be the one who got hit by the Dillons and then lucked out with the Shaws, and you only got dumb nuns like a thousand live-in baby-sitters? Maybe if we'd been together all along . . . like we should've been! We should've been!

Call me up, she thought. Call me. Call me. She rolled on her stomach and stared at the phone on the bedside table. It was a trimline Princess phone. I don't know your number. I don't know where you live. You know where I am. Call me up. Call me.

She was so ready to pick up the phone that when it did ring, she grabbed it before a full loud jangle could be heard out in the backyard. "Hello, Alice," she whispered furiously.

"You have to shout," said Alice. "I can't hear over these things."

They made a plan. Alice still had five bucks left from the talent show prize money. She would come back and ask Mr. and Mrs. Shaw to adopt her. How could they refuse her? Saturday would be a good time. Mr. Shaw would be home from work, and everybody'd be relaxed and in a good mood. "Have you got that?" said Miami, trying to shout softly. "I think come at ten. Then we can talk a bit at the bottom of the steps and plan it better. I knew you'd call."

"Sister John Boss isn't going to like this very much," said Alice. "But who cares?"

"See you then," said Miami. "Sis."

"So long," said Alice. "Bye." She didn't hang up. She wasn't very good at the phone, Miami realized.

"Hang up now, someone's coming," said Miami, and did so herself.

"Who're you shouting at?" asked Garth.

"None of your beeswax, nosy."

"You got grass stains all over the bedspread."

"I'll get grass stains all over your face if you don't watch it."

"Oh, yeah?"

"Yeah."

Garth considered. "Oh. Boy, we didn't get very far with our plan, did we."

"Not yet," said Miami, "but just wait."

On Saturday morning Miami finished her chores early and said, "I'm going outside."

"Don't go far," said Mr. Shaw, turning the pages of the *Times Union*. He lost himself in the columns usually, chuckling out loud at the funny ones. Miami was surprised he had even heard her. "We have a family outing planned as soon as your mom gets up and has her breakfast."

"Oh, no!" said Miami. "Why doesn't anybody tell me these things? What're we doing? I don't want to go."

"We're taking a drive over to Troy," said Mr. Shaw. "We're going to go see Alice and have a chat with Father Kevin and Sister John Bosco."

"What time?"

"About midmorning. When we're ready."

This was awful! This was a disaster. Alice might be sneaking away just as they were driving over to where *she* lived. But Miami couldn't really say she didn't want to go. Maybe they were going to make an offer to adopt Alice. Maybe they'd listened to Miami. Taken her seriously. For once.

If Alice showed up in a taxicab before they left, well, they could just drive her back. Miami went out to wait at the foot of the steps.

Mrs. Jenkins was there scrubbing her sidewalk with a brush and disinfectant. She was so weird. "Miami Shaw," she said in her raw voice. "Where in the world were those clergy taking you the other day?"

"It wasn't me," said Miami. "It was my sister, Alice."

Mrs. Jenkins had to know everything. And Miami was so nervous, waiting for Alice, that she told her the whole story. "Well, that's one for the papers, that is!" said Mrs. Jenkins. "Your folks going to call a press conference?"

"What's that?"

"Where you call the newspapers and radio and TV chan-

93

nels and tell them all to come at a special time. Then they hear you make a speech and tell the world your unusual story. And yours is a doozy, it is. A lalapalooza."

"Well," said Miami," I don't know about things like that."

"It'd be front page of the papers, I bet," said Mrs. Jenkins. "Did you ever hear the like?"

"I better go in now," said Miami. "Garth needs help tying his shoes."

"Such a nice sister to Garth, you are," said Mrs. Jenkins. "I know. I see what I see. Well, you'll get over it."

Oooh, the witch. Miami ran up to the house.

Then adult forces took over, pushing the kids this way and that, the way they always did. The babies howled. Garth was goody-goody, eager to see this Alice again. Miami kept running to the tower to stare down into the street, looking for a taxi. But none stopped, and before too long the family had bundled into the Rust Queen, Mr. Shaw's name for the '61 Chevy deathtrap they risked life and limb in, or so Miami thought. Alice was not in any taxi they passed so far as Miami could see. She dreaded the scene when they got to Troy.

But despite herself, she grew interested in seeing where Alice lived. She hadn't been to Troy before, or not that she could remember. In school they called Troy the armpit of America. It didn't look so bad to Miami. And with Mrs. Shaw craning for landmarks and Mr. Shaw cursing (or as near as he came to cursing) at the one-way signs, Miami had ample opportunity to imagine that *she* lived in Troy, and Alice was her sister in Albany somewhere.

The Sacred Heart Home for Girls loomed like a red brick office or factory. The area around it seemed slummy. Miami had been expecting a private house with a picket fence and gaily painted shutters, a garden with big floppy flowers. But the home shot up three solid floors into the air like a fortress, like a massive land formation. It was flat-topped, with iron grille in the lower windows and bars on the top ones. Were they to keep girls from falling or from jumping, Miami wondered. "Creepy," said Garth. That just about summed it up.

Sister John Bosco opened the front door. Father Laverty was in a sitting room off to one side, looking hot and peevish in his black clothes. He bulged inside them as if quilted there. He was fanning himself with an issue of *Catholic Digest*. A statue of Our Lady, with a chip in her foot, presided from a side table. A plate of homemade cookies and glasses of lemonade waited on a tray. The chairs were a thousand years old, straight and flat and dark and horrible; they made you repent just to look at them. "Won't you have a seat," ordered Sister John Bosco. "I'll get Alice." Father Laverty, Miami noticed, had taken the only upholstered chair for himself. She couldn't blame him.

Then it was "Father Kevin" and "Joe" and "Joan" and "the little ones," chummy as a cocktail party. Miami blanked out for a while, imagining that Sister John Bosco would return on the run with news that Alice was nowhere to be found.

"But what a name, Miami," Father Laverty was saying to her. "There's no Saint Miami in the community of saints, as you well know."

"Yeah, where did my name come from?" Miami had never asked before.

"She was Carol before," said Mrs. Shaw. "We had a lot of advice on how to adjust her ideas of family life when she came to us. She was in a bad way. Doesn't remember much of it, do you, dolly?" She smiled. "So we gave her a new first name and shifted Carol to a middle position, and since we weren't sure, we invented a new birthday to mark a new beginning for Miami Carol Shaw."

"But Miami?" pressed Father Laverty, sneaking a glance at his watch.

"That was my mother's maiden name," said Mrs. Shaw. "I was adopted, too. We wanted to build the sense of family history. My mother died a few years ago, but while she was alive she loved Miami very much, and the name is now passed on."

"I sound like a football team or an airport," said Miami.

Then Sister John Bosco returned, calmly, quietly, steering Alice Colossus by the shoulder.

Alice shrugged at Miami. "Couldn't slip away. Too many nuns around," she said, or that was what Miami guessed she had said.

Sister John Bosco passed around the cookies and lemonade. Fanny and Rachelle were set on the floor to gnaw at the legs of the beastly chairs or whatever else they could get into. "Now we're all together again," said Sister John Bosco. "The second of many such meetings, I'm sure. Will you start, Father Laverty?"

The priest stared at his cookie as if asking it for guidance. Then he looked around at each of them, a nice uncomplicated look into all their eyes, and said, "We're here for two reasons. We're here to understand why Alice Colossus is not Alice Shaw, and why she can't be, won't be. It'll take a long time to understand this, and today is just a beginning. We also need to invent some ways Alice Colossus and Miami Shaw can come to know each other as sisters. As twins, in fact. They will be in each other's lives from now on, for as long as they live, and nobody is going to stand in the way of *that*. So this day's work is partly hard, and may involve some tears, and partly joyful, because the hand of God and the surprising initiative of Alice have pulled the cloak of mystery away from our eyes."

Miami almost murmured, "Amen," but controlled herself.

Father Laverty went on with such delicacy, such gentleness, that at times Miami couldn't follow. But the gist of it seemed to be that there wasn't a snowball's chance on a pancake griddle anyone was going to let Alice get adopted by the Shaws. First, there was money. Then there were the laws of the state of New York. There were Miami's needs as a preteen recovering from nasty early years she could hardly remember. There were Alice's special needs. There was Garth to think of, and Fanny, and Rachelle. It turned out Alice had had a chance for adoption already this year, first time ever, and she'd turned it down.

"But that don't count!" interrupted Alice, her first public pronouncement. "The Harrigans! It was right after Sister Vincent de Paul got burned up! I made a pact with God!"

"Oh, you did," said Father Laverty, more kindly than ever, so softly Alice couldn't hear him and looked bewildered.

"*Oh you did,*" intoned Sister John Bosco helpfully into her left ear.

"Yeah, I did. I said when Sister Vincent de Paul comes back safe and sound, I'll do whatever. I'll pack up and go anywhere. But not till I know." Alice had a fierce look, a look of a guttering candle, or of a bird banging against the insides of a window, not knowing why it can't go through. "I said I won't go to the Harrigans till after Sister Vincent de Paul shows up! And she never does!"

"The point is," said Father Laverty, "that Alice is making leaps and bounds this year. Her misbehavior has its positive side, and though Sister John Bosco loses sleep from time to time, I feel quite comfortable in Alice's development." Sister John Bosco was shooting him such an onslaught of disapproving looks that he amended his remarks quickly and said, "Of course I only get the most limited of pictures. Sister John Bosco, have you anything to add?"

"Let us remember," said Sister John Bosco, "that we're not here to deprive anyone of anything, but to give our children the best chances they have at success. Some of the children start with considerable disadvantages. Alice is one. Learning to disobey—I feel compelled respectfully to correct Father Laverty—is not a sign of advancing maturity. On the other hand, look what Alice *has* achieved this year. Her taking part in the spring musicale by playing Eliza Doolittle was a triumph—not just of her willpower, but an aesthetic success as well. Alice is a gifted singer, even with her disabilities, and may be very proud of how she has marshaled her talents and her confidences."

Sister John Bosco then went on, "And it is not lost on anyone here that Alice's pact with God implies a seriousness, a sobriety of moral purpose that is all too lacking in the young in this day and age. Her commitment to Sister Vincent de Paul is further proof of her accomplishments. Alice has come out of a private harbor, where once she verged on autism, to care deeply about herself and the world. Alice," she turned, and a lovely smile blossomed within the frame of her wimple and cowl, "we will do all we can to turn you loose on the world with a vengeance, packing six-shooters if you must. But even if adoption by the Shaws were a possibility—which it is not—I could not recommend it for you. You need more exclusive attention still than the Shaws, however devoted to you, could provide. Do you understand what we're saying?"

"I can't go," said Alice in a thick voice.

"You're not even invited," said Miami with bitterness. "This is a party to celebrate your being left out. Care for some more lemonade?"

"I can see the family resemblance," said Sister John Bosco tartly.

"Let's move on, shall we?" said Father Laverty. "I have to coach a CYO baseball game in Latham at twelve-thirty."

For a while then they talked about what *could* be done. Next summer Alice and Miami might go to Camp Saint Theresa during the same session. Maybe they could talk on the telephone once a week, on Saturdays? "For a predetermined length of time," said Sister John Bosco. Maybe monthly visits? "How about Christmas?" said Miami. "There are some things the grown-ups should decide in private," Sister John Bosco remarked. "But this is a healthy start. Would the Shaws like to see the home now before we all get on with our busy days?"

"Yeah," said Garth. "Come on, Alice, show us where you sleep."

"But just a minute," said Mrs. Shaw, gathering up babies from the antiseptic floor. "Did I miss something, or is Alice still in the dark about this nun in the fire? This Sister Vincent de Paul?"

Everyone looked just a bit uncertain.

"Well, it's clearly significant," said Mrs. Shaw, apologetically but also boldly. "Sounds as if Alice wants to know, and she's old enough to deserve the truth, I suppose. Did the nun die?"

"Well, of course not," said Sister John Bosco. "There would have been a requiem mass, and the girls all would have attended."

"She's not dead?" said Alice.

"Alice," said Sister John Bosco slowly, "where in the world did you get the idea she might be dead?"

"Well, where *is* she?" said Alice. "It don't look like she's around anymore, so where is she?"

"Oh, my Lord," said Sister John Bosco. "It never occurred to me you didn't understand. I'll tell you, I need a month off. Alice, look at me. Listen to me. Sister Vincent de Paul is very much alive. She is recovering still. She's getting better all the time. I don't know if she'll

come back here. She's no spring chicken, you know."
Alice's eyes clouded over at this, and Sister John Bosco
said, "I mean she's an old nun now. In fact she's been an
old nun most of her life. She's taking her sweet time to
recover, and then we'll see what we see."

Miami saw Alice's face turn white then red: joy and
sorrow, sorrow and joy. "You mean she's alive," she kept
saying. Miami was just faintly jealous. Here they should
be united in fury at the grown-ups ruining their lives, and
Alice's face kept looking like the last two minutes of a
Christmas special on TV. "Come on, show us your room
so we can get outta this place," Miami said brusquely.

Behind Alice, Sister John Bosco was gushing. "You
never know with her. She's so sharp about some things,
and then the basic bit flies right by her somehow. I can't
thank you enough for seeing what I had missed, Mrs.
Shaw. God bless you."

Part Five

O CLEMENT O
LOVING O SWEET

Alice was in the chapel.

A grab bag of joys, curses, and requests was trying to fold itself into the shape of a prayer. She felt as if she had a circus in her head. It made her tired, and as she knelt she rested her forehead against the back of the next pew and her fanny on the edge of the bench. Sister Paul the Hermit, passing through to hunt for a lost handkerchief, saw her there. To Sister Paul the Hermit, Alice looked like a girl trying to apologize for making so much trouble. There was a keen smell of lemon Pledge from the pews, and tiger lilies brandished their blossoms from plastic buckets. Someone had left a duster on the lectern. Sister Paul the Hermit swooped up to retrieve it, casting a glance at Alice as she went, in case Alice looked as if she needed to talk. Alice didn't meet her glance.

Alice's gaze went back and forth between the two paintings in the chapel, one over each of the wrought-iron racks of vigil candles. The painting on the left showed Jesus tenderly pulling aside His robe to reveal in His chest a heart wreathed in thorny twists of vine. It was a sort of spiritual X-ray painting, because the bleeding heart didn't seem to drip blood on the white garments. Alice felt a sort of affection for the Jesus of this painting, more so than for the emaciated body of Christ hanging on the cross above the altar. After all, this was the Sacred Heart Home for Girls. And the look on the face of Jesus in the painting was affecting. He looked shy, and honest, and a little bit embarrassed to admit He'd gone through all this trouble just for people. He reminded Alice of that boy with the guitar she'd met on the bus, about whom she'd dreamed once or twice.

The heart didn't seem so awful. It wasn't a horror-movie thing. It was God's heart, but it was like Alice's heart too. Hearts were really magnets, weren't they? Her heart seemed to twist in her chest. It strained and rested and strained again, chained not by thorns, but by love and need and desire.

O God, did I do wrong? she prayed. Should I have gone off with the Harrigans last winter? Would none of this then have happened? Is this mess with Miami Shaw just punishment for my bribing You to save Sister Vincent de Paul?

No, said Jesus. I don't punish people for loving each other.

I wish I believed You, prayed Alice.

It don't make any sense, said Jesus. After all, the Harrigans probably would've sent you to Camp Saint Theresa just like they sent Naomi Matthews. You still would've learned about Miami this summer either way.

Alice hadn't realized Jesus was so logical. So this mess *wasn't* a penance for being willful. She felt a little better, and politely put Jesus on hold while she turned her attention to the painting on the right, which was of Mary. Long practice at this had taught her Jesus didn't mind waiting, airing His sacred heart in silence.

Mary hung in a cloudy sky, her hands out, her feet gingerly arching, her face oval, and her hair mostly hidden in a veil. Her expression was more inward, and it always took Alice a longer time to get through to her. Mary was full of grace. She was blessed among women. There was a line from a prayer they repeated daily, a line that the girls enunciated with special fervor, so even Alice understood it. "O clement, o loving, o *sweet* Virgin Mary," they trumpeted, "braa na na na na na . . ." and on into obscurity. Alice used "O clement o loving o sweet Virgin Mary" for her icebreaker whenever she prayed to Mary. Sooner or later she got Mary's attention.

First she adored Mary for a few minutes, never being quite sure how much was too much. She apologized for her failure of nerve. She gave thanks for the good fortune she'd had and prayed for better in the days to come. Mary cast her eyes humbly to the floor.

The real point of all this, concluded Alice, is what to do now?

Mary said nothing, as usual. She waited for you to figure it out for yourself.

I mean, now that Sister Vincent de Paul is alive again—

105

still alive, I mean—I could be brave enough to be adopted, but nobody wants me now. The Harrigans have Naomi Matthews because I wouldn't go. That Shaw family has Miami. Now that I have to act brave to keep my end of the bargain, there are no options.

There's a bravery in waiting, said Jesus from the other side of the room.

Mary smiled inwardly. Well, you wouldn't expect her to contradict her son.

I thought it would be a little harder, said Alice. I already know how to be patient.

What do you love most of all? said Jesus. The first, best thing?

You, said Alice.

Not counting me, said Jesus; I mean from the world.

I love Sister Vincent de Paul, said Alice, and her heart twisted again, slid against itself, burning. She's still alive, said Alice, though Jesus of course knew all. And the tears burned in her eyes like her heart flaming in her breast. It was joy and loneliness together, that's what it was.

Should I ask her what to do? Is that it?

Jesus said, Pray for her, Alice, and keep your ears open. The right thing will present itself.

I'm part deaf, Alice reminded Him.

I know, He said. You know what I mean.

Alice signed off, gratefully, flicking a quick glance at Mary, who seemed to be smiling more lovingly than ever. There really is satisfaction in prayer, Alice thought as she genuflected and took off down the hall toward the dormitory. Chapel's the only place where grown-ups don't make you repeat yourself. You can be understood the first time.

She sang as she changed from a cotton skirt and blouse to shorts and T-shirt. She didn't exactly know what to do next, but she was going to keep her ears open, and maybe the right thing would occur to her.

Sister John Bosco was reviewing the food order for September when the phone rang. Putting her pencil on the line that said *Jell-O—50 packs assorted flavors*, she shot a "hello" into the mouthpiece. First there was no sound, then a giggle. Then a high voice being pushed into the alto range by willpower said, "Hello, is this Alice the orphan's house?"

"With whom do I have the pleasure of speaking?" said Sister John Bosco, faintly amused.

"What?"

"Who is this please?"

"Oh. Umm . . . umm . . ." A muffled conference, then: "This is Mister Joe Shaw."

"I see. Well, Mister Joe Shaw, Alice can't come to the telephone. May I take a message?"

"What?"

"What do you want me to tell her?"

"Tell her—tell her—" Hysteria overcame the speaker, and the line went dead. Sister John Bosco replaced the handset, shaking her head, but paused a moment later with her pencil at 2 *cartons Carnation evaporated milk*. She was not immune to the sound of giggling children's voices and appreciated the anxiety that encouraged children to misbehave. Heaven knew she had accepted the role of principal of the home because of her savvy with kids as well as an adroitness at administration. Her first duty in this case was to Alice, of course, but she could imagine what Miami and the malleable Garth—and the well-meaning parents, for that matter—would be going through, too. She would have to pray, and reflect, and hope for guidance. She would not allow a serious interruption to the progress Alice had made this year, however, as who knew what trials lay in wait for her outside the gates of the home.

She crossed out *10 packages Oreos* and scribbled *fresh fruit* next to it.

In the evening she made the rounds to be sure all the girls were calm, bedded, prayered, and reading. She held Ruth Peters for a while and took away a water gun from Esther Thessaly. She noted a broken screen on the third-floor landing, chastised Sister Francis Xavier gently on an abundance of bath water on the tiles, and perched for a minute on the edge of Alice Colossus's bed.

"Who was our father and our mother?" said Alice, looking up from a Dr. Seuss book she ought to be well beyond at this point.

"God is our Father," said Sister John Bosco automatically.

"I know," said Alice, "but the other kind. The real kind."

Sister John Bosco resisted the temptation to plunge into a discussion on the nature of reality. "I don't know," she said, which was the truth. "Your mother could not feed and raise you herself, so with great love and forethought she gave you to us. She knew you'd be safe and well here. She was very smart and loving to do such a kind thing for you. What're you reading?"

"Horton Hatches the Egg," said Alice. "I like it."

"That's a book you could read three years ago," said the nun. "I thought you were up to Nancy Drew."

"I meant what I said and I said what I meant," said Alice.

"An elephant's faithful, one hundred per cent," said Sister John Bosco. Call and response. Well, there was something faintly psalmlike about Dr. Seuss. She kissed Alice good night. "Oh, by the way, that little boy, that Garth, was put to the telephone and spoke with me today. I tried to tell him we weren't in the habit of calling our children to the phone, but I don't believe he understood."

"Funny little kid," said Alice. "I like boys."

"So do I," said Sister John Bosco. "Sweet dreams."

During the pancake breakfast next morning, a Sunday after-mass tradition, Alice scooted out to the front hall and used the phone again. Mrs. Shaw answered but put Miami on anyway. Alice said to Miami, "It don't look like anything's going to work."

"I have an idea," said Miami. "Wait, I'll go upstairs where I can shout louder. Mom, put this phone down when you hear me upstairs, okay?"

Mom, thought Alice.

Miami's voice reappeared a minute later. She launched into a breakneck explanation of what they could do. It took Alice, straining to hear, some time to get it straight.

It involved calling up local TV stations and radios and having a press conference. They could do it on the steps to the Shaws' house at South Allen Street. "Twins Reunited," they could say. Some neighbor of Miami's had given her the idea. Miami was obviously gaga over the scheme. She had worked out what they could wear. Could Alice get her ears pierced by next Saturday?

"You are out of your mind," said Alice. "Nobody has their ears pierced here. We get a little cologne at Easter. It smells like Ivory liquid. That's it."

Miami was even less happy to learn that Alice wouldn't do it. "What's the point?" Alice asked.

"Shame the filthy grown-ups into letting us live together."

"I can't shame the nuns," said Alice. "I don't want to."

"I can shame anyone," said Miami, "including myself."

"I'm impressed," said Alice, which made Miami laugh, which made Alice laugh, and they were really sisters.

Alice knew the breakfast would be over soon, and some nun would come out and find her. She thought fast and suggested they write a letter to the newspapers instead. "Let's not shame anybody," said Alice. "Let's just explain what happened and we can thank the Shaws and the nuns for taking care of us."

"What good's that going to do?" said Miami.

"It won't be a secret anymore," said Alice. "Nobody can go back to pretending we aren't sisters. No matter what happens."

Miami grunted and tried to persuade Alice about the press conference again, but Alice balked. She could be stubborn. Miami finally caved in. She would write the letter and sign both their names to it, and send it to the *Times Union* and the *Troy Record* and maybe the *Evangelist*. Alice said "Okay, bye," and hung up fast. Sister Ike gave her a dirty look as she barreled along, but didn't utter a word.

The letter appeared in the paper the following Saturday. Alice found it with pride and dread, read it, and ripped out the whole page before anyone else could see it. She folded the letters column to the size and thickness of a stick of Wrigley's spearmint gum and carried it around in her shoe. Only in the lavatory did she let herself open it and read it again.

Dear Mr. Editor,

We are two girls named Miami Shaw and Alice Klossos, aged 12, exactly *the same age. We both went to camp this summer and found out we were twins and we never knew it. We look alike except I have pierced ears and Alice has longer hair. I am adopted and Alice isn't, she lives in Troy with some nuns. We are happy to the nuns and the Shaws for taking care of us but* we don't ever want to be separated. *This is a matter of some interest to the people of Albany I do think.*

MIAMI SHAW and ALICE KLOSSOS.

PS: I like Beetle Bailey but why do you waste space on Steve Canyon, he isn't funny and nobody reads it.

*   *   *

Alice thought Miami was a very good writer. She didn't even mind so much that her name was spelled wrong; maybe then nobody at the convent would ever hear about it.

The newspaper was set on the side of Sister John Bosco's desk, atop two weeks' worth of newspapers. When the phone rang and the caller identified himself as a reporter referring to an item in the letters column, Sister John Bosco flipped the paper open. (Alice didn't know the principal received her own private subscription.) Under a heading "PARENT TRAP" COMES TRUE? OR LITTLE WHITE LIES? she found the letter. "I am astounded," said Sister John Bosco, who rarely was.

"Is it true?" said the reporter. "Or is there another orphanage run by nuns in Troy? The chancery wouldn't release that information."

"No comment," said Sister John Bosco smartly, and hung up.

So the trouble Alice and Miami had concocted got thicker and stickier. The following day the newspaper showed a photo of Miami Shaw on her front steps, and underneath ran a caption: "Letter Writer Claims She's Discovered an Unknown Twin; Diocese Refuses to Comment." A short article nearby hinted delicately at the powers of twelve-year-old girls to invent fabulous tales. Apparently Mr. and Mrs. Shaw would only say, "Miami is our true and legally adopted daughter and that's all there is to say about it."

112

Sister John Bosco's curt, "No comment," looked suspicious and incriminating in print.

And a day later a guy jumped out from behind a phone booth when Alice and the others were walking two by two to get some new school shoes for the fall. He stuck a camera in Alice's face and blinded her momentarily, and by the following morning the story had moved up to the front page. They reprinted the photo of Miami, and next to it showed Alice looking wide-eyed and bleached out. The caption read:

SEPARATED AT BIRTH—SEPARATED STILL

Alice rather expected a crackdown of security at the home, and she was right to expect it. Small metal digits, like stacks of nickels, were inserted in the telephones to prevent anyone without a key from dialing out. The daily newspaper no longer appeared in the wreck room. Sister Paul the Hermit began locking the door into the kitchen with a key, so that no one could get in or out unless she was there. There seemed to be a nun on the horizon from morning to night, wherever Alice was inclined to walk.

For all that, there was no lecture, no accusation, no request for an apology, no penance. Sister John Bosco told Alice minimally what was going on. "Such shenanigans do no one any good," she claimed, "least of all you. You aren't to blame for anything, Alice, and you have nothing to be ashamed of."

"So when do I get to be trusted again," said Alice.

"What is *not* to be trusted, and this is significant," said

Sister John Bosco, "is how people might twist and use what you might say innocently to harm you. Even without your knowing it. They have no right. And I'm afraid your sister did a dangerous and stupid thing to write to the newspapers. However, it will all blow over soon. Some train wreck or drug raid will come up to distract everyone. It can't be easy for you."

Sister John Bosco never asked Alice if she had sanctioned the letter, or even written it herself. Apparently the misspelled last name was enough to persuade the nun that Alice's name was used without her knowledge or consent. Alice did not enlighten her.

And the nuns did not censor the mail. "I don't believe in opening other people's correspondence," said Sister John Bosco, handing Alice several letters each day. Since, however, Alice had no stamps and no way to get to any, there wasn't much danger of an extended correspondence. Alice showed everything to the nun.

The letters were mostly from older women, some of whom had lost children in the Vietnam War or in accidents. They filled their peach and lavender notepaper with Catholic pep talks. But one lady had grown up at Sacred Heart herself, and she told Alice it had been a living hell. "Poor soul," murmured Sister John Bosco, reading over her shoulder. The nuns were Nazi commandants, wrote the woman. Get out while you can.

"How sad to be so bitter." Sister John Bosco sighed. "Before my time, alas, or I'd go and wring her wretched little neck." Alice stared in horror, but Sister John Bosco was grinning a wry ribbon of a smile. It was a joke.

114

Then one day there were two pieces of mail, either one of which had the power to jump start Alice's life had it been in danger of running down.

The first was from Sister Vincent de Paul.

Dear Alice,

I hear from my spies that you are in the middle of a pickle of some sort. Be a good girl and pray for guidance. Always remember Jesus loves you and so does Sister Vincent de Paul, though I have lots less influence. Sometimes a storm comes and the thing to do is wait it out. A sudden calm can be as surprising as turmoil, shocking even, if you're used to commotion. Are you still doing speech therapy? Keep it up. I'm doing a set of painful leg exercises, but there's not much point. I would like to see you someday before I die. I am mostly better and miss my girls in Troy and my kitchen. The food here is not food at all, like the macaroni and cheese they served at lunch, well let me tell you the macaroni was all dried out and the cheese had gone home. Ah, well, I'm waiting it out, too.

> *Yours in Christ,*
> *Sister V. d. Paul*

"If you'd like to drop Sister Vincent de Paul a note I'll be happy to post it for you," said Sister John Bosco.

"Mmmm," said Alice noncommittally, awash in relief and terror.

The second piece of mail, in the same magic batch, was a postcard. It read:

Dear Alice Colossus:

All the stories in the newspapers and that one photo they keep running: I can't get it out of my mind. Are you the same girl I sang on the bus with, that day last winter? Seems like a miracle. My name is Larry Deeprose. I'm a student at SUNY, phone 555-6713. Give me a call.

Your friend,
Larry

"This one can't be for you," said Sister John Bosco, evidently forgetting Alice's misbehavior last February. "I'll toss it."

"No, I like the picture," said Alice cleverly, flipping it over to show (thank you, Jesus, that there *was* a picture) a photograph of a statue of Moses in some park. "I like Moses."

"Very well," said Sister John Bosco, and went on to supervise someone else's life for a while.

Alice was in the chapel again. In her lap were the letter from Sister Vincent de Paul and the postcard from Larry Deeprose. She didn't know if she was there to pray, or just to be alone. It was late afternoon, and she could hear the girls in the yard outside playing volleyball. The sounds of girls shrieking at volleyball did not seem out of place in a chapel, to Alice's surprise.

It was as if her life had woken up again. Well, she didn't have parents, she didn't have Mr. and Mrs. Shaw and those cunning baby girls, and adorable Garth, and feisty Miami as a companion and cohort. She didn't even have the Harrigans. What did she have? She had the nuns, same as ever, not so bad, better than a lot. And now she had Sister Vincent de Paul again. But she was dying! There wasn't much hope! She wanted to see Alice again!

O clement o loving o sweet, began Alice. Mary smiled privately, as usual; Jesus showed His heart, as if to say but hearts still can be broken, you know. I am always here. The light filtered in through the waxy colored windows. A bus belched out on Fifth Avenue, and the diesel fumes made it into the chapel. I want to be a nun, thought Alice. Keep your ears open, Jesus advised again; there's plenty of time for all that.

And about the boy with the guitar—Larry Deeprose. Deeprose! If there was a more romantic name for a student to have, Alice didn't know it.

She began to add things up.

A few days later Sister John Bosco handed Alice a stamped envelope on which she'd written Sister Vincent de Paul's address, a place in Glens Falls fitted out for old or recuperating sisters. "You *have* written your best old friend a note?" asked Sister John Bosco. Alice nodded. "And I'll mail it on my way to the store," said Alice. "Sister Paul the Hermit Crab wants me to go to help her carry stuff back."

"Sister Paul the Hermit Crab?" Sister John Bosco raised her eyebrows almost up to her wimple.

"You must've heard me wrong," said Alice, blushing.

"You know how bad I talk." She fled with the envelope. Inside it she slipped a piece of paper with lots of tiny writing on it. First she copied over Sister Vincent de Paul's address on a separate scrap of paper, so she'd know it; then she crossed out the address on the envelope and wrote Miami's address beside it. That afternoon she slipped the envelope in the mailbox.

THE SNOW PEOPLE

Sister John Bosco threw open the window of her office. Fall had swept in overnight, and a tide of cool, forgiving air spread through the city streets. Moisture in the atmosphere, rising damp from sidewalks and tiny front yards. The tang of an alley skunk. She inhaled with gusto and noted with pleasure that Father Laverty was late. Two minutes of grace, two minutes to do nothing but receive the fall like a guest into her office. It was Saturday, the girls were off picking apples, all but Ruth Peters, who'd begun misbehaving lately, and Alice Colossus, who was having her once-a-month outing with the Shaw family of Albany. Sister John Bosco broke a crust off her morning roll and sprinkled the brown bits on the windowsill, admiring the birds. She gazed at a poor woman in a tattered housecoat plowing slowly through the first fall of leaves and wondered briefly about the ragged woman's child-hood.

When Father Laverty came bustling in a moment later, Sister John Bosco was at her desk with a file in her hand. "You're late, Father," she said tartly.

"Traffic, I overslept, moral inferiority—pick your excuse," he said. "Are you going to eat the rest of that roll, or is it going begging?"

They settled down to work. Finances out of the way first, then a few legal questions about the diocesan opinion on various kinds of group health insurance. Sister John Bosco ticked off the items they'd handled on a small, white pad. They came to Alice.

"You will know that the annoying newspaper attention has given rise to all sorts of difficulties," said Sister John Bosco. "I've had no fewer than five women contact me claiming they gave birth to twin daughters at Brady Memorial in nineteen fifty-six, and threatening legal action to reclaim Alice."

"So what's the problem?" said Father Laverty. "Maybe one of them is telling the truth. Or maybe one of them would make a good mother for Alice anyway."

"*Five* of them aren't telling the truth," said Sister John Bosco, "or we'd have a miracle on our hands. Besides, the records at Brady Memorial show that *no* twins were born to unwed mothers in nineteen fifty-six. So clearly all five women are lying, or deluded. This isn't a sound basis on which to begin considering their fitness to adopt one of our girls, as you well know."

What was it about him, Father Laverty wondered, that

caused Sister John Bosco to speak like a state legislator? Perhaps he should come to these meetings in his day-off garb and leave the collar at home.

"*No* twins at Brady that year?" he queried. "So what sort of miracle are we really talking about here? Where'd Alice and Miami come from then?"

"The records show that they were found abandoned in the hospital lobby on June twentieth. They were a week or ten days old. There is no evidence anywhere that names either parent, and none has ever come forward to Brady Memorial to claim responsibility. Nor, might I add, has any of these five women made the slightest suggestion she had the twins elsewhere and delivered, or arranged for the delivery of, the babies to the maternity hospital."

"So the nuts have come out of the woodwork," he observed.

"Where the press is concerned, they usually do," she said.

"What is the long-range hope for Alice Colossus?" said Father Laverty after a while. "I rather like her, you know."

"Well, of course you do. She's quite a thrilling child in her own way. Her early disadvantages aside, she's pushing forward out of herself with commendable spirit. It appears she may be bright enough after all, though that's been hard to determine so far."

"The hearing? The speech?"

"The hearing seems to come and go. Dr. Bradford suspects it isn't as bad as Alice makes out, that perhaps it's a trick of the mind. The hearing gets worse in times of stress. But the speech is improving all the time. It's a small problem, really, compounded in part by the hearing and in part by an overgrown integument at the back of the tongue. We are advised that minor surgery when she's fully grown may help correct the pronunciation of the broad vowels, the fricatives, the labials . . . the works."

"And is she ready to leave us? If the right set of parents came along?"

"Well, who can say?" Sister John Bosco allowed herself to look uncertain. "We make the best decisions we can. But what hangs in the balance!" She went on to explain. "I have just heard from the Harrigans, that couple who wanted Alice last winter, only Alice wouldn't go. They took Naomi Matthews instead. They're having a terrible time with her and want to send her back here."

"What sort of terrible time?"

"Naomi is thirteen. What sort do you think?"

"What do you propose? Do you want to send Alice there now?"

"We're not a hotel, nor are we a lending library of children," said Sister John Bosco. "We don't circulate our wards at the whim of cardholders in good standing. Should Naomi herself make a request of us to come back, I would not turn her away, naturally. But the Harrigans need to spend some time learning to be good parents. Six months is not enough."

"You'd make a good mother," said Father Laverty daringly.

"I *am* a good mother," she retorted. "Now next on the agenda is Ruth Peters."

*　*　*

Alice, Miami, and Garth were sitting on the porch rail. Alice and Miami were waiting for their worst misbehavior ever to start. Three times while spending Saturday together they'd already gone through the litany of comparisons and sized each other up and marveled at their similarities and differences. Miami couldn't sing to save her life. They were both great at basketball. They both had allergies to tomatoes. They both had gone to the memorial service for Dr. Martin Luther King, Jr. What if they'd seen each other there! But they hadn't; there was such a crowd. They couldn't figure out which one of them was smarter, which made them both feel relieved.

Miami said to Garth, "We're not doing anything exciting today, so you're not invited."

"She's my sister too," said Garth. "You can't disinvite me."

"We can go in the ladies' room, and you can't follow us there," said Miami.

"What ladies' room?"

"We'll find one someplace."

Alice sat holding the wallet she'd made for Sister Vincent de Paul during the summer. Usually she was nice to Garth. Today she was too preoccupied to pay attention to him. Miami hoped Alice knew what she was doing. Whatever trouble they got into today, Miami knew *she'd* be forgiven. The Shaws bent over backward to forgive. It was dumb, really, but there was no point in letting their wishy-washy goodness go to waste. With nuns, however, could forgiveness ever be relied upon? No matter what

Alice said, Miami's experience in school seemed to suggest otherwise.

"Garth," said Miami, "if you're really good to us and leave us alone today, I'll let you go up in the tower room."

He scowled. "When?"

"Whenever you want."

"Hah!" he said. He knew an outright lie when he heard one. Miami amended her offer to give it more credibility. "Well, whenever you want if I'm not there or if I am and I don't care."

"Like right now?"

"Well, yeah," said Miami. Garth scratched his behind. "Only don't fall out the window. It's awfully high."

"I'm very good at balancing," said Garth, and darted away to take full advantage of the permission.

"Come on, let's go," said Miami, looking at her watch. "They'll be back from Westgate Shopping Center in a little while. I've left the note to say we went to Patty's."

"Should we leave Garth alone?" said Alice.

"We shouldn't," said Miami, "but we're going to. Don't worry. I'll ask Mrs. Jenkins to keep an eye on him. The old bat, she's always snooping and prying anyway, she'll love it."

Mrs. Jenkins seemed so amazed at the sight of the similar girls that she agreed without so much as a snort. "Get that Garth to play on the porch," she said. "I'll watch him while I'm putting in my tulip bed."

Father Laverty had stayed for a bowl of minestrone and then tootled off to the alcohol rehabilitation ward at Saint

Peter's to say an early vigil mass for the patients. The girls came back from apple picking, boisterous, cheeks as red as the bushels of fruit they hauled in from the station wagons. Ruth Peters stopped crying and began to behave. Sister John Bosco was called in by Sister John Vianney from the basketball hoop in the backyard, where she was playing a little one-on-one with the older girls. She adjusted her veil and went to the phone in the lobby.

It was Mr. Shaw on the phone. Miami and Alice were missing, but not to worry.

"You left them alone in the house?" cried Sister John Bosco, incredulous.

"We thought we had to show them we trusted them," said Mr. Shaw.

Sister John Bosco released a force of air from between her lips that, had it been interpreted into English, would have required her to confess to profanity. "Where might they be?"

"Well, we called Miami's friend Patty, where they said they were going. But Patty's mother said Patty was away for the weekend, and she hadn't seen them at all. And we called some other friends, and the library, and no one has seen them. They're probably just walking around the neighborhood. I'm sure of it, in fact. But I wanted to let you know."

"You let Miami walk around the neighborhood alone?"

"This isn't Fifth Avenue in Troy, Sister," said Mr. Shaw, a little sharply, "and Miami *has* lived here for seven years. I wouldn't be inclined to worry except they left Garth here alone instead of taking him with them, which is what they were instructed to do. I only bothered to call in case you had any ideas."

Sister John Bosco's mind began to race. What if one of the women who'd come to claim Alice had been making inquiries, had figured out from the phone book where the Shaws lived? What if she'd been stalking around waiting to cause trouble? It was farfetched; it was even faintly hysterical. But she'd rather be accused of hysteria than allow harm to come within an inch of the twins. "You'd better call the Albany police," she said evenly, "and maybe the state police as well. This could be trouble."

Mr. Shaw said to his wife, "I'm *not* going to call the cops. It's Saturday afternoon. Alice has been here three times already, and the girls have giggled and horsed around like ordinary kids. That they disobey right now is just part of the game. They have to test us, to see whether two of them are stronger than we are. Sister John Bosco is being excitable."

"But Alice *is* her responsibility, ultimately," said Mrs. Shaw. "And we should be seen to be cooperative, for Miami's sake, in the long run. For all our sakes. I suppose it won't hurt to call."

So Mr. Shaw phoned, apology for bothering the police reeking from him like cigar smoke. Garth sat on the blanket with the little girls. He was afraid he'd misbehaved, that it was his fault. He didn't want Miami to get in trouble.

He watched his mother. She fussed with making hamburger patties for freezing, rounding each one perfectly, with the daunting confidence grown-ups had at everything they did. She smacked the finished burgers flat on squares of waxed paper she'd cut with pinking shears. She looked completely calm. When Mr. Shaw came back from the phone, she said in an even voice, "Did you tell them what Miami was wearing?"

"How do I know what Miami was wearing?" he snapped.

"She went with you over to Troy when you picked up Alice," she snapped back. "It could be important. Call them back. Levi's and a pink corduroy jacket. And Alice in a plaid skirt and a big, blue, oversize sweater, a nun's cardigan."

"They're identical twins, for heaven's sake," said Mr. Shaw. "You could hardly get a better identifying feature than that."

"Call them back," she said, banging an aluminum mixing bowl on the edge of the counter.

Well, Garth thought, it was time for him to leave. He went up the stairs in bewildered grief, resting both feet on each tread before continuing. He didn't know why they had to *fight* about it. They never fought. If he hadn't agreed to stay home this would never, never, never have happened. Somehow it was all his fault. He couldn't tell exactly how, but he felt as if he were wearing iron clothes, as if his feelings were crushed by them.

Maybe he could see them from the tower window.

He brightened up a bit and the iron feeling left his clothes. He made it up the ladder to the dusty chamber, sunny under the inverted cone of the ceiling. He looked out this way and that. He could see Saint Peter's from here! And all the way down into Mrs. Jenkins's yard. Maybe if he sat on the edge of the window he could lean just a small way over and see farther up and down South Allen Street. They'd be awfully glad downstairs if he found Miami and Alice.

The window was unlocked. It swung inside on hinges that squeaked.

He didn't much like being *too* high, he decided.

But it was awfully important to find Miami and Alice, wasn't it?

Sister Francis de Sales sat with Sister John Bosco in the office. The other nuns had taken the girls off on their Saturday afternoon walk to the Troy Public Library. The place was quiet again. Sister Francis de Sales had given up trying to be comforting, as Sister John Bosco seemed to find comfort irritating just now. They simply sat, waiting for news.

"You don't *know* what a trial it is," said Sister John Bosco, as if Sister Francis de Sales had just claimed such knowledge with insulting possessiveness. "These children are loaned to us for a time, loaned by God. They're like our own talents, like the talents in the parable, Sister. We are required to preserve them and allow them to grow and develop. Yet there are wolves disguised as saints out there, not even knowing themselves what they are, waiting to snatch up our precious talents and diminish them. Do you know what I'm saying, Sister? Do you understand what I mean?"

Sister Francis de Sales wasn't at all sure what Sister John

Bosco meant. But she nodded piously. "Yes, Sister." She was grateful that the phone rang just then.

"What," bellowed Sister John Bosco into the phone.

Her eyebrows lifted, her hand trembled a bit. Sister Francis de Sales continued the rosary under her breath. She'd been working on it silently since Sister John Bosco had begun to ramble. Sister John Bosco picked up a pencil and said, in an unctuous tone, a *pretty* voice that Sister Francis de Sales had never heard before, "Well, I'd very much like to meet you, Mrs.—is it Mrs. Coyne? Mrs. Patrick Coyne. May I call you by your first name? Mary. And a number?"

"Holy Mary Mother of God," intoned Sister Francis de Sales, "pray for us sinners now and at the hour of our death. Hail Mary, full of grace . . ."

"You have reason to believe you may have information relating to our little Alice. Perhaps we should set up a meeting, shall we? Have you a street address, then, Mary?"

". . . the Lord is with thee. Blessed art thou amongst women, and blessed is the fruit of thy womb, Jesus," prayed Sister Francis de Sales, noting that Sister John Bosco was affecting an Irish accent. She rounded the outer limit of the rosary beads and began on the fourth decade.

"A lead," breathed Sister John Bosco, hanging up the phone and closing her eyes. "Maybe it's nothing. But this lady calls and says mysteriously she might be related to Alice. I'll put the state police on this right away."

"Sister, haven't a number of people called with that suggestion?" asked Sister Francis de Sales.

"It's the timing, Sister. This one sounded serious, and

we have to follow every clue." Sister John Bosco sniffed. "She might have Alice and Miami with her right now. We'll treat this with kid gloves until we know more. Now say your prayers!" She dialed the police for the fourth time in an hour.

Sister Francis de Sales obeyed, observing mildly to herself that she could well understand why the girls called this woman Sister John Boss behind her back. ". . . now and at the hour of our death," she prayed, Alice surfacing as the focus of her intentions. Alice Colossus, be careful. Be careful!

Garth was holding on very, very tight. South Allen Street went on and on. He was such a little boy, really; even he knew that. He was just beginning to figure out that he was going to grow up. One day he'd be like Mr. Shaw, only he'd be a fireman and a rock star and a king like the black king who died last spring. Being halfway out on the roof made him feel small, made him smell the distance not just between himself and the sidewalk a million miles away down there, but also between himself and being grown up.

If he fell he'd be smashed to smithereens, into pieces as tiny as the ants he liked killing.

"Mi-A-mi," he called. His voice flew, high and melodic, over tar roofing and through yellowing leaves. "Mi-A-mi! Where ARE you?"

A movement! He craned to see. He reached, he stretched, his butt shifted on the windowsill, his sneaker heels dug into the rain gutters.

It was only Mrs. Jenkins. As Charlie Brown said all the time: Rats! She had heard him. She came poking her nosy head over her fence, where she'd been fussing around with her old stupid flowers. She belted out like Carol Burnett doing Tarzan, "GARTH SHAW! YOU GET RIGHT BACK IN THAT WINDOW BEFORE I COME UP THERE AND SMACK YOU!"

Old busybody witch, thought Garth, and reached to obey.

The car slowed down. It was a street of broad lawns and grand old houses, anchored by huge, overweight stone porches. This much farther north, the trees were flushed with red, scarlet, crimson, gold, orange, salmon, and pear yellow. The lawns were flawlessly raked, empty of fallen leaves, AstroTurf green. A black cat sprang along on legs stiff as Popsicle sticks.

"Number two-forty-two. There it is," said Miami. "Boy, are nuns rich or what?"

"Corpus Christi Home for the Retired," read the boy, the traitor, that Larry Deeprose. "This what you want?"

"This what you want, Alice?" asked Miami, running her hands through her hair for the ten-millionth time in an hour. Alice, in the backseat, didn't speak.

"I said," said Miami louder, turning around, "here we *are*, Alice."

"She's expecting you. Should we wait outside?" said Larry. "Or go get an ice cream and come back in an hour? You want to be home by five, we'll have to get back on the Northway by four, I think." He turned to look at Alice again. "Hey, you're worried. You want us to go in with you? She *is* expecting you, isn't she?" In his treachery he was more beautiful than ever, eyes glinting like the mica in the glass cases of the State Education Building. "Say the word."

"No," said Alice. "I'll go in myself. Go away."

"Go *away*," hissed Miami, pretending it was a joke, falling with fake laughter against Larry, who shifted apart from her a little. "That's a good one."

"Go away," said Alice, and got out of the car. She held her wallet in her mouth, smoothed down the front of her skirt, reclipped her barrettes.

"Let's go find the waterfall they named Glens Falls for," said Miami. "C'mon, Larry."

"Alice," said Larry, leaning his face on the triangular bracket made of the crook of his arm resting on the open window. "Alice, you sure you don't want us with you? You look terrible. We're doing this for you, you know."

She turned. Miami was almost in Larry's lap, her face poking out the window like a violently colored balloon. "Oh, well," said Alice, "wouldn't it be loverly?"

She went up the slate sidewalk alone, Larry's "Well, Miami and I will be back at four then, sharp," ringing rather precisely in her ears, each syllable making its own little click, like a billiard ball slotting into its pocket with neat efficiency. The black cat, which had taken up a pose of elegance, released itself after a bug, hurtling into the air with an ungainly, splayed look. It made Alice think, hard-heartedly, that cats had fur, too, so why weren't there cat pelts, like rabbit skins, on sale?

A girl hardly older than she opened the door. "Sister Vincent de Paul," said Alice. "Please."

"It's their nap time," said the girl, who was obviously an after-school helper. "Come back later."

"I can't. There isn't any later," said Alice.

"But you have to," said the girl, looking as if she cried a lot and had gotten used to it. "You interrupt their schedules, and they're a crazed lot. Takes days to calm everybody down."

"But it's me," said Alice. "Alice. It's Alice. Her Alice."

"Oh," said the girl, convinced of something by the tone in Alice's voice. "Well, wait here, and I'll see if I can wake the dead." She disappeared down a bright corridor with huge windows making up one wall, and on windowsills below, rangy geraniums, whose alarming blossoms were clots of fire-engine red all the way along. Alice waited. Miami and Larry Deeprose had canceled each other out in her mind, Miami falling for Larry's tender good looks and Larry for Miami's chattery brashness. So Alice was back where she started nine months ago. Today only high winds passed over the Victorian houses in Glens Falls, but she remembered the simultaneous snow and rain of last February. To live in the world, it seemed, was to be always caught in a grip. A stranglehold of opposing forces. Loving and needing. Staying and going. Doing right and committing wrong. What had she learned from bribing God to save Sister Vincent de Paul? Only that one could still feel betrayed by a miraculous new twin and a flattering boy-man. Alice was still paralyzed, with only herself to rely on.

Ah, said Jesus, a surprise mystery guest in the front hall of the Corpus Christi Home for the Retired. Where two or three are gathered in My name, there I am.

With Miami Shaw and Larry Deeprose and me? thought Alice. You could hardly be more insulted than to find Yourself among the likes of us! Me sulking in the backseat! So cross and so disappointed! Larry blithe and friendly, as kind to Miami as he'd been to me, as if there is no difference between us! And Miami so ugly, so coy, so flirtatious. A tramp! Hogging the front seat just because she'd followed the instructions I'd sent her in that letter and called Larry to set up this whole elaborate plan!

Still, said Jesus, I didn't lay down any conditions. You three came together to do something good, to see Sister Vincent de Paul before she died.

Oh, said Alice to herself, not a prayer, almost a curse: Faith is so *maddening*!

"You're in luck," said the girl. "I peeked in. She's awake and seems to be whittling or something. Come along, but quietly."

Down the geranium hall. Up a couple of steps. Through a swinging door.

A room, number eight, with a big, broad door wide enough to fit a rolling bed through. The girl put all her weight against it, and enough of a crack appeared for Alice to go through. "Go on in," said the girl, "she's still alone this week. Mrs. Lambrusco croaked in August." She tittered nervously and fled.

Alice squeezed through.

Bereft of veil, an ancient figure was spread with white

sheets instead of black sleeves and skirts. Her hair was cropped like an old man's, gray and thinning, though a froth of curls hazed up the front of the scalp. She was pushing little numbered squares in a black plastic frame, trying to organize something.

"Sister," said Alice.

She looked up. She threw the toy on the floor. Her mind wasn't dead. "Alice Colossus," she exploded, "what for the love of mike are you doing here?" She threw the sheet aside, and Alice was in her arms. Who rocked whom would not ever be clear to Alice, as long as she lived; but they rocked back and forth, Alice half kneeling on the hospital bed, getting a cramp in her left calf, crying and weeping and sobbing and sniffling and laughing and hiccuping and laughing some more.

After a while Sister Vincent de Paul said, "Get me my housecoat from the hook, there, and we'll go down to the sun room at least. It's still nap time, so all the old ninnies will be snoring away. We can sneak in some talking time before the boob tube starts blaring away again."

"This one? The one with the roses?" said Alice. "It don't look like anything I thought nuns could ever wear."

"Alice, what's happened to your speech," said the nun. "You've been practicing just to delight me."

"No, I haven't," said Alice, delighted.

"Well, I don't believe you. Yes, that's the one. Silly froufrou ruffles. Alice, whatever else nuns get wrong, we have the right idea when it comes to a life without ruffles. Now let me take your arm, sweetheart."

"Sister Vincent de Paul," said a nurse in the hall, a

stringy woman buttoned into an antiseptic uniform the color of Listerine, "it's resting time."

"I'm making a prison break; my girl has brought me a file in a cupcake," said the nun. "Get out the German shepherds. Alice, meet Nurse Khan. Nurse Genghis Khan."

"I'll get you yet, Attila the Nun," said the nurse, moving on with a tray of thermometers. "Beware, beware."

"Revenge is sweet, saith the Lord," said Sister Vincent de Paul.

She and Alice reached the sun room without further roadblocks and settled in a wicker settee upholstered in material printed with loony psychedelic flowers. "Now, Alice, tell me everything in the world. On your mark— get set—go."

"No," said Alice. "You first. Are you dying?"

"Eventually. I've let my language rip too often to be able to ascend bodily to heaven. I've got to take the conventional ground transport: grave first. I never minded second class. You meet more interesting people there."

"You don't look like you're dying."

"I'm only old, Alice; I'm not antique. Did someone tell you I was on my last legs?" She lifted her twisted foot an inch or two. "This has been my last leg since I was one day old."

"But you wrote me," said Alice, flushing, with relief and embarrassment. "You said you wanted to see me again before you died."

"Well, and so I have," said the nun, "and if God sees fit to give me an all-expenses-paid trip to Rio during the carnival season I'd also be grateful." She peered at the girl. "Oh, Alice, 'Before I die'—that's an expression the old use! It's sentimental claptrap! I didn't mean I was *dying*!"

Feebly, anticlimactically, Alice whispered, "Oh. Good. Okay."

"The young are so literal," said the nun. "That's not their fault, but it's a pain in the neck sometimes. No sense of irony. Well, live and learn. I should've known. You've been thinking I was a done thing. My word, I *am* sorry. Stupid me. Now you, Alice. What's what. Tell me all about this twin thing. Is it true?"

"I'm not sure I want a twin anymore," said Alice, and haltingly explained. Halfway through, Sister Vincent de Paul held up a hand. She turned and yelled down the hall, "Nurse Nero! Put down your fiddle and come be useful!"

The nurse arrived, scowling. Sister Vincent de Paul said sweetly, "Would you please make a few phone calls for me? My little friend has made an error in judgment and come forty-five miles unchaperoned with a strange man in a car."

"He's not a strange man!" cried Alice.

"Trust me, that's how they'll see it, and well they should," said the nun. "He's an idiot to have believed you and Miami. He should've talked to the Shaws before agreeing to drive you anywhere. Give the young the vote and wheels, they forget what responsibility means. It's this new permissiveness; I don't think much of it. Nurse, call and tell the Shaws that the girls are here and listen to what they suggest."

The nurse said to Alice, "Could you please get her mother superior to come and pick her up? She has no business being retired. She thinks she's a captain of industry and I'm her private staff. Call yourself," she said to the nun. "You know where the phone is."

"I can't stand that long and you refuse to put in an armchair," said the nun. "And Alice can't hear over the phone."

"I can now, sort of," said Alice.

"Well, start being grown-up then and call them yourself," said Sister Vincent de Paul. "It won't be fun, I guarantee it, but you'd better do it."

After a nightmare conversation with Mr. Shaw, full of surprise, rage, worry, and relief, Alice came back to the sun room. Sister Vincent de Paul was napping in the sun. Alice didn't have enough time left to be courteous. She woke her up.

The nun blinked twice. "I had a lovely nothing of a dream," she mumbled, and then shook her head. "Now what were you doing?"

"I called Mr. Shaw," Alice reminded her.

"Ah yes. The father. And?"

"He's driving up here," said Alice. "He wasn't very pleased with us."

"Good. Then he's a good father for Miami," said the nun. "Now, Alice, what about you?"

"What about what about me?"

"Well, those people who wanted to try you out. The Hoosies. The Harrigans. You said no."

"I said not yet," said Alice, but didn't explain her bargain with God.

138

"And now they have our model girl Naomi."

"She's turned into a big pain," said Alice.

"Excellent. Good," said Sister Vincent de Paul. "It was about time. But Alice, that means they chose Naomi instead of you. Do you mind?"

"Yes," said Alice, surprising herself. "Yes. They should've waited. Why do I get all the bad luck? Look at Miami! There we were, twins, and someone came along and adopted her—not once, but twice! She had a family till she was six, and now the Shaws! She's got good ears, and she don't have a fat tongue. She's got two sisters and the cutest little brother you ever saw. And her mom is pregnant. She's got pierced ears and a room in a tower and a boyfriend named Billy. And she's busy taking over Larry too. We started out the same, and look: She got the lucky life and I got zilch."

"Now Alice," said the nun. "You don't have zilch. Tell me what you have. Come on. Count your blessings."

"I got Miami as a sister," said Alice sullenly. "I got no parents, no family. I got cheated."

"Hah!" said the nun. "You have a lovely voice, a brave character, a steady faith. You have the gift of being loyal to your old friends. You have food daily, and clothes, and a roof over your head. And the sisters to love you and take care of you. What more do you want, you greedy thing?"

"I want a miracle," said Alice. "I thought finding Miami and the Shaws was a miracle. But it isn't."

"Honey child. Now you listen to me. The whole thing is a miracle, Alice. The whole shebang! The strange twists of fate, the heartache, the snap crackle pop of everyday life. Come on! The sun out there on the metal trash cans!

139

The yeasty behavior of that Nazi nurse. You have to ap-
preciate it, though, Alice. Don't go pushing it off because
you have some picture of somebody else's life in your
mind. You've got to grab it, whatever it is comes down
the pike, you grab it. With both hands."

"But look at you," said Alice. "How would you know?
You're a nun."

"That's right, that's what I grabbed," said Sister Vincent de Paul, "and I never looked back. And I'm a nun
like no one else, for which my superiors offer novenas of
gratitude. Alice: The miracle is that you *can* grab. It's not
what."

"You mean it don't matter whether anyone wants me
or not."

"No. That's not what I mean. Of course it matters. But
while it's mattering, your life seems to be to live at the
home. So grab that. It's a real life—an unusual one, but
a real one. If some other choice comes up—and it will,
believe me, sooner or later—and you choose it, choose it
with gusto. But mind the details! Miracles are everyday
stuff, Alice. No shortage of them."

"Miracles are magic," said Alice. "God's magic."

"Baloney," said the nun. "I don't believe in magic."

"If I could only see just one miracle," said Alice.

"You're my miracle. My very best miracle of the whole
day," said the nun. "And tomorrow there'll be another."

"There was snow and rain on the same day!" exploded
Alice. "The day the retreat center burned down! And you
got burned and almost died! That's a *miracle*? You grabbed
that with both hands? Miami got a family and I got nothing!

I'm supposed to be happy God puts us through stuff like that?"

"Ah, Alice." Sister Vincent de Paul drew herself up and reached for Alice's hand. "The storm. The snow. Did you ever hear, Alice, did you ever hear people say that no two snowflakes are alike?"

"How could I? What people say don't come through."

"Now you're being petty. Tell me the truth."

"Yeah, I heard it. But who could ever check all them snowflakes to be sure?"

"It's the idea. A snowflake, Alice. Listen. A snowflake begins in the air. It's like a tiny life. Think of two snowflakes formed at the exact same instant, an inch apart, Alice. They drift and tumble and float to earth at the same time. But the wind, the heat or cold of the air, the particles of dust or whatnot that they encounter, each little thing that happens to them helps in the shaping of them. They grow differently. They respond by growing a molecule this way, a molecule that. Maybe ten minutes go by. They're unique in the whole universe."

"So," said Alice. "So what."

"You and Miami are twins," said Sister Vincent de Paul. "You have some things in common maybe. But your paths through the air are entirely different. Your characters are maps of things that happen to you, in a way. We each have our own path to take. Don't begrudge Miami hers. She didn't choose it any more than you chose yours. I didn't choose to get burned. But since I couldn't prevent it, Alice, I at least accepted it. I don't blame myself or God for it."

"You're not making anything any easier," said Alice.

"Alice, we're all like snowflakes. We're snow people. If you try to live someone else's life you'll never be happy. You have to live your own."

"But what is my own?" said Alice.

"If I had all the answers, I'd be the president," said the nun. "You have to find it yourself. But if you don't do it with a good heart and an open spirit, you'll waste a lot of time."

Alice sighed. She sat digesting the idea that things weren't going to get much smoother. Then she remembered the wallet. She handed it to Sister Vincent de Paul. "I made it for you at Camp Saint Theresa," she said shyly. "Even though I thought you were dead."

"Now that's faith," said the nun. She was very pleased. She admired the bright red stitching. "I can keep my holy cards in here. Oh, I see you had the same idea. But Alice, I don't have anything to give back to you."

"It's okay," said Alice.

"I *can* tell you this," said the nun. "The new kitchen wing on the retreat house has just reopened."

"But I thought the retreat house burned down."

"Only the back wing and part of the chapel. That crazy storm was bad in icing over the roads, but it helped control the spread of the fire. The insurance money covered the renovation."

"Oh," said Alice. They were silent for a minute. "But you never explained one thing. How can we be grateful God does fires and makes us orphans and all? I still don't get it."

"Oh, well," said the nun, "here come the old biddies for their game shows. We can't talk about such things in front of them; they'll just get depressed. They aren't as brainy as you and me." She winked at Alice. "Besides, some things you have to save to ask God. It's one of the best things to look forward to about dying."

They sat for a while, holding hands, not talking.

The sun turtled its way across the sky, and the shadows slowly lengthened. A deeper blue came into them, and slanting light caught a congregation of leaves fluttering in the strengthening wind. The nurse came through with paper cups of apple cider and handed Alice one too. It was sweet and brown and thick as syrup, the first scrumptious cider of the season.

By the time Miami and Larry returned, Mr. Shaw and Garth had already arrived. Sister Vincent de Paul, wrapped in her roses and flounces, had progressed to the front hall, and they were all waiting there together. When Miami saw her father, she drew in a breath and said, "Uh-oh, it's my dad."

"Oh, hi," said Larry, holding out his hand. "Pleased to meet you."

"If you ever come near these girls again," said Mr. Shaw, "I'll break both your legs. You'll be lucky, young man, if I don't press charges for kidnapping. Don't you dare try to shake my hand—I won't answer for my actions."

"What?" said Larry Deeprose, appalled, incredulous. *"What?"*

"You heard me," said Mr. Shaw. "You'd be smart to keep your distance, young man."

"Look," said Larry, flustered, "look. You—I don't—there's a terrible misunderstanding."

"Daddy, you're embarrassing me!" said Miami. "Oh! I'm *so* embarrassed!"

"The kids said it was a family crisis, and they needed my help," said Larry. "I thought I was doing a favor—I never—I wouldn't—"

"I'll deal with them," said Mr. Shaw, "but you're either innocent to the point of stupidity, or you're a fool. Get out of here."

"Daddy, I'm going to die of embarrassment," cried Miami. "Don't be so *mean*! What do you think this is, a crime show on TV? He's just a friend of Alice's! We were just coming to see this old nun Alice is so dotty over."

"I don't suppose a cup of tea all around would help?" said Sister Vincent de Paul. "I thought not. Well, Alice, then I'll say good-bye. Remember, mind the details. Even of this." She hugged Alice tightly and held the crown of Alice's head in her left hand. "Go with God and the angels."

"Thanks, you too," said Alice. And they had moved out onto the stone porch before she could think of anything better to say. Larry Deeprose was inside, still mired in flummoxed phrases of explanation. Mr. Shaw propelled the girls before him, a hand on each of their necks.

"*You* called Daddy?" guessed Miami, hissing at Alice. "You rat fink."

On the way south to Albany the girls both sat in the backseat, as far away from each other as possible, staring out opposite windows. Garth sat in front with Mr. Shaw, who as he drove delivered himself of a nonstop harangue that was just as furious at Alice as it was at Miami. This was the last straw. This was the living end. This took the cake.

This is family life, thought Alice, hardly minding a bit. Soak it up while you can.

Part Six

THE MIRACLE

The first snowfall of the season came, an early one. Sister John Bosco stood with her hands behind her back looking out at the streets. The dismissal bell had rung a bit ahead of schedule, and the girls in their hand-me-down snow-suits and parkas and jackets were making a merry racket in the school yard. Beyond, the normal view of Fifth Avenue was thickened and bleached with the squall. Traffic was moving slowly. A number of fender benders would occur, no doubt; they always ushered in the winter.

She was waiting for the Coynes. Most likely the snow had held them up. This was too bad. Sister John Bosco had planned to release Alice to them while the girls were still at their lessons, to avoid protracted good-byes and difficult, maudlin scenes. But now there would be the mess of sympathy and grief to deal with. Ah, well.

When she saw the Coynes, inching along on the slick pavement, having parked perhaps over on Congress Street, she felt a thrill of relief. She hadn't quite allowed herself to admit that she was afraid they'd be no-shows. And Alice with her suitcase packed, sitting in the cold hallway all this time.

Mrs. Coyne, Mary Coyne: a woman in her forties, bland, intelligent, restrained. How wrong to have imagined her as a potential kidnapper. For after Mr. Shaw had called to explain where the girls were, Sister John Bosco had had to swallow her pride and apologize to Mrs. Coyne. It turned out that Mrs. Coyne had had some theory that the twins might've been the daughters of her estranged younger sister, who had died in unfortunate circumstances not long after giving birth. An analysis of all the facts on hand, including blood tests, proved this to be a false lead.

But while the blood parents of Miami and Alice were still a mystery, and likely to remain so, Mrs. Coyne's interest in Alice proved to endure beyond the inquiry over the facts of birth. She and her husband had applied to take Alice for a trial period. The marriage was strong. Mr. Coyne worked for the state budget department. They were regular parishioners of Saint Thomas in Delmar, and the pastor there had given excellent references. Alice would be only a few miles away from Miami, and they could continue becoming friends and sisters after the punishment period was over. Mr. and Mrs. Coyne seemed sensitive to the complexities of Alice's needs, and of their own.

They drew nearer. Mr. Coyne with two bunches of red

roses in his arms! Mrs. Coyne's straight black hair hidden by a scarf. The snow blotting them from view, revealing them again, teasingly, capriciously.

"Alice, please come in," said Sister John Bosco into the hall.

"They changed their minds, I know they did," said Alice, entering. "No. Did you change yours?"

"No." But the girl looked terrified. Thin and eager and pale as the snow. She'd labored over abandoning little Ruth Peters, who had fits of screaming whenever the subject of Alice's leaving came up. Sister John Bosco had had to take great pains to point out that it would be wrong for Alice to allow the cries of Ruth Peters to keep her from this opportunity.

"I want to say something to you, Alice," said Sister John Bosco. "It is something I say to all my girls when they leave. I say it to the little ones who won't remember. I say it to the girls who graduate and go on to live elsewhere for high school. I say it now to you, and I mean it as deeply as ever I've meant it."

"Well, say it," said Alice, jiggling a little; through the high icy windows she could see the Coynes approaching.

Sister John Bosco jettisoned the homily about God being the real home of all souls. She bypassed all the sub-themes about elevating obligation over devotion, maintaining the sterling reputation of Sacred Heart girls, and keeping sacred the sanctuary of the Holy Spirit, which was to say Alice's developing human body. She said, "Alice, I love you. We all love you, and we always will."

"Oh," said Alice, standing on one foot, then on another.

Then she put both feet down. She turned her head and peered at Sister John Bosco. "How can you love all of us? There's so many."

"It's a miracle," said Sister John Bosco. "The heart has infinite room inside it." She never talked like this. "Now straighten up and let me look at you. Have you your handkerchief? Have you our phone number in your purse? Do you have your rosary?"

"I knew there were miracles. That's what I said to Sister Vincent de Paul," said Alice. She was chattering. "Do you think we'll have a snow day tomorrow? Ruth would love to make a snowman." Oh, but tomorrow she'd be in a new life. She paused, flustered.

"We'll make a snowman with Ruth," promised Sister John Bosco.

Sister Francis of Assisi knocked and entered. "Sister, Mr. and Mrs. Coyne are here," she announced.

"Show them in, Sister," said Sister John Bosco.

Dripping snow onto the threadbare Oriental rugs, they came inside. They were ceremonial, shy, and flushed with high color. "Sister, for you," said Mr. Coyne grandly, presenting a bouquet of roses in a sodden mass of pastel-colored paper. "And Alice, for you."

"How lovely," said Sister John Bosco, whipping her handkerchief from her sleeve and blowing her nose. "I shall put them at the altar of our Blessed Mother, and we will be reminded to pray for your continued happiness."

Alice looked a little hidden behind her clutch of blossoms. "Ow," she said, "thorns." Then she laughed. "Details," she continued, almost to herself.

"Shall I call the children inside?" said Sister Francis of Assisi. "To avoid a scene? Although you know what they'll be like if we don't let them stay outside until suppertime. The first snow and all," she explained to the Coynes.

"Might you postpone leaving a bit?" asked Sister John Bosco.

"The roads, Sister," said Mrs. Coyne, "they'll only get worse. And we've a lot of settling in to do tonight." She smiled at Alice, who stared down into the roses, blushing.

"Well, then, Sister, you just have Sister Isaac Jogues take Ruth Peters inside for a few minutes to warm up," said Sister John Bosco, anxious at least to avoid the worst scene of all. She had already withheld from Alice the information of Sister Vincent de Paul's stroke and quiet death last week; she would do everything she could to launch Alice as confidently as possible. "And now if we're ready? Alice, button up," she said.

But Mrs. Coyne was already bending over, wrapping the scarf around Alice.

So Alice walked with roses down the long, dark hall, to where Sister Francis of Assisi, Sister Francis de Sales, and Sister Francis Xavier stood flanking the broad double front door. Both sides of the door were opened to add to the ceremony, and a square of blowing snow showed beyond. Mystery, adventure, and hope. Between the Coynes, Alice stepped out into the world. The girls in the school yard saw her go, and clambered up the short rise to the inside of the fence, calling *Good-bye, good-bye,* and the nuns behind them waved like mad, their black veils slowly turning white with the drifting of snowflakes.

151

Gregory Maguire, like Alice Colossus in *Missing Sisters*, spent some time in a Catholic home for children when he was small. He was born and raised in Albany, New York, where he went to college, taught grade school, and founded a folk choir in his parish church.

He is the author of fantasies, science fiction, and picture books for children, and he is a popular speaker at professional conferences and at schools in the United States, Canada, England, and Ireland. He received his Ph.D. from Tufts University and now divides his time between Boston, Massachusetts, and London, England. A founder and codirector of Children's Literature New England, Inc., Gregory Maguire is also a composer, an artist, and an avid traveler. His most recent journey took him to see the castle of Count Dracula in the Transylvanian Alps.